EVERYONE WAS BARFING EXCEPT TORI!

Closing her eyes, Tori held the bag in front of her. She shook it gently and softly began to recite the poem:

Belch, burp, puke,
Slobber, spit, spew.
There is not a single thing
That you can do.

Suddenly the air was filled with the sounds of people gagging and throwing up.

All over the room kids were vomiting onto their lunch trays! Teachers were throwing up into their sandwich bags! Everyone was barfing all over the tables! Upchucking onto the floor!

A terrible stench filled the air. Tori's stomach was doing flip-flops. She grabbed her nose and rushed toward the door, too.

She stopped at the swinging doors and looked back over the scene. It was incredible! The cafeteria and everyone in it was a total mess. Tori was the only one who wasn't throwing up!

Read all of the BONE CHILLERS from HarperPaperbacks:

#1 Beware the Shopping Mall
#2 Little Pet Shop of Horrors
#3 Back to School
#4 Frankenturkey
#5 Strange Brew
*#6 Teacher Creature**
*#7 Frankenturkey II**

*coming soon

BONE CHILLERS

STRANGE BREW

BETSY HAYNES

HarperPaperbacks
A Division of HarperCollins*Publishers*

HarperPaperbacks *A Division of* HarperCollins*Publishers*
10 East 53rd Street, New York, N.Y. 10022

First printing: July 1995

Printed in the United States of America

HarperPaperbacks and colophon are trademarks of HarperCollins*Publishers*

❖10 9 8 7 6 5 4 3 2

For my friend Tori Pardo, her brother Max,
and all my other friends in the American School
of Madrid, Spain

Chapter 1

"What do you mean you're going away for the whole summer?" demanded Tori Pardo.

She and her best friend Heather Hartner were walking toward school on a bright June morning, and Tori stopped in the middle of the sidewalk, staring at Heather in disbelief.

"Isn't it exciting? My grandmother has invited me and all my cousins to visit her in Florida," said Heather, chomping on a wad of pink bubble gum. "She lives in a house on the beach, and she has a boat, and she's going to take us to Disney World. It's going to be such a great summer!"

Tori thought her heart would burst. Heather was going to have the most wonderful summer anyone could imagine, and she would be stuck with nothing to do in tiny Domburg, Illinois, population 750. Even the nearest shopping mall was twenty miles away!

Tears welled up in her eyes. *How could you do this to me?* she wanted to shout. Instead, she dug a tissue out of her jeans pocket, blew her nose, and asked glumly, "When did you find out?"

Heather looked sheepish. "I've known for a week, but I didn't know how to tell you. Gosh, Tori, I wish you could come with me."

"Fat chance," muttered Tori. She blinked away the tears and looked imploringly at her best friend. "But honestly, Heather, I'm going to *die* if I have to spend the summer all alone."

Heather sighed sympathetically. "School isn't out for three more weeks. And even then it won't be so bad. There are . . . well . . . lots of things to do," she said lamely.

"Name one," said Tori. Already she could see herself sitting in her room and staring out her window across the cornfields day after endless day. To make matters worse, Heather would probably send her tons of postcards from Disney World!

"You could hang out at the mall," offered Heather.

Tori shot her friend an angry look. "You know I can't do that. How would I get there? With my mom working, it's always *your* mother who drives us to the mall."

Heather didn't say anything for a moment as the girls walked on toward school. Suddenly she brightened and said, "But you're going on a vacation next month, aren't you?"

"Our trip's canceled! We can't go anywhere this summer because of my stupid brother."

"Max?" Heather asked. "He's only nine. What could *he* do to change your plans?"

Tori scowled. "He made the Little League baseball team, that's what!" she said. "And now we can't take a trip because the coach says if anyone misses one single game, he's off the team. So what if it ruins *my* summer? My parents don't care. They worship Max!"

"Oh, Tori. Stop exaggerating," scolded Heather. "You know they love you just as much as they love Max."

But Tori couldn't help feeling envious of Max. She still remembered when he had been a newborn baby—her parents had been so busy taking care of him that they seemed to have forgotten all about her. Tori had invented an imaginary playmate she had named Celeste to keep her company. There hadn't been many girls Tori's age nearby, and Celeste had become so real that she and Tori had been constant companions, playing together right up to the time in third grade when Heather and her family moved to town. After that, Tori hadn't needed

Celeste anymore. She had forgotten all about Celeste and had never even told Heather that she existed.

I wish I still believed in Celeste, Tori thought with a sigh. Then my summer would be fun, even though Heather won't be here.

As they walked along in silence, Tori thought about Heather. It always amazed her that two people could be such opposites and still be best friends. Heather was tall and freckled with curly red hair. Tori was small, olive-skinned, and her shoulder-length dark hair was smooth and straight.

But that wasn't all that was different about the two girls. Tori loved to be where the action was. She hated sitting around watching other people have all the fun and get all the glory! She dreamed of being a star. She wanted to do something exciting and glamorous! Something a zillion times more adventurous than sitting around all alone for the entire summer watching the corn grow in dull old Domburg.

Heather, on the other hand, was quiet and practical. So sensible. She never took wild chances or got involved in harebrained schemes the way Tori did. Heather's idea of a good time was working on her stamp collection. Why was she the one to get to spend the summer in Florida when I'm the one who would really know how to live it up? Tori wondered.

Still, Heather was special. Having her for a best friend was like having a second conscience, Tori thought and smiled to herself. More than once she had kept Tori from getting herself in deep trouble.

"Tor-ri . . ." came a soft, whispery voice. "Tor-ri . . ."

Tori looked around quickly. Who had said her name? It had sounded like a girl, but it wasn't Heather. She was blowing a pink bubble as big as her head.

"Tor-ri . . ."

Tori spun in the other direction. Maybe someone was hiding behind a tree and trying to scare her. Maybe it was Ted Kinner, imitating a girl. He sat behind her in class and was always getting into trouble for playing tricks on other kids. Well, she'd show him. She'd pretend she didn't hear him.

"Tori Pardo. Look!" The voice was louder this time.

An eerie feeling came over her. Heather hadn't heard the voice, and Tori felt as if some mysterious force was turning her head and focusing her eyes on the trash barrel at the edge of the school yard.

Lying beside it on the ground was an old red spiral notebook. At first Tori thought someone had pitched it toward the trash and missed. It lay in the dirt, crumpled and dog-eared.

She thought it looked strangely familiar. Then she noticed the writing on the cover.

PROPERTY OF VICTORIA PARDO
KEEP OUT
THIS MEANS YOU!

Tori gasped. It was *her* notebook! What was it doing here? She had thought it was at home, safely hidden in the back of her closet. Had Max been into her things again?

I'll murder him! she thought, stooping to pick it up.

But Heather had spotted it, too. She was closer to it than Tori and she bent down, scooping it up first.

Tori held out her hand. "That's mine. Can I have it, please?"

She held her breath, praying Heather wouldn't open it. It was a kind of diary, and there were things in it she couldn't show anyone. Not even Heather. Mostly it was filled with gripes and frustrations about how her parents paid more attention to Max than to her.

In her notebook she had written secret plans to get even with Max. Like putting superglue inside his baseball mitt so his fingers would be stuck inside and he'd miss his turn at bat.

But it also contained an entry about how she wished she had a friend besides Heather. She had written it one day last winter when she had been mad at Heather for refusing to go sledding with her in the park. Tori had been dying to go, but Heather had said it was too cold, she had the sniffles, and she wanted to read a book. The feeling of being lonely and abandoned had come back to Tori, and she had poured her heart out to the notebook, describing how she longed for a friend she could have wonderful adventures with—someone who would be a lot more fun than boring old Heather.

Now she was sorry she had put that in her notebook. She wished that she had torn out the page and thrown it away. She hadn't meant a word of it. Not really. She had only been upset.

I'll die if she reads it and thinks I don't like her anymore! Tori thought desperately.

Heather grinned mischievously and held the notebook out of Tori's reach. "What's the big mystery? Is it full of secrets?" she asked gleefully.

"Just give it to me," Tori demanded. It was better to let Heather get angry at her than to let her see what she had written.

Tori thought for a second that Heather was going to hand it over. But instead, she flipped through the pages.

"What's the big deal?" she asked, sounding puzzled. "There's nothing in here. See? All the pages are blank."

Tori blinked in astonishment. She took the notebook from Heather and slowly turned the empty pages one by one. What had happened to her notebook? How could all her secret entries have disappeared?

Then she noticed that one page wasn't blank. It was the very last page. And the writing wasn't hers.

"Look at this," she said, pointing to the page. "It's really weird."

"It looks like a . . . a recipe," said Heather.

"Yeah, but look. It's a recipe for . . . a *storm*," Tori said.

Both girls stared at the page in amazement.

Chapter 2

As Tori read the strange recipe her scalp prickled as if a hundred spiders were dancing in her hair.

To cook up a fierce storm with roaring thunder, streaking lightning, and howling wind, gather the following:

1 cauldron
2 round smooth stones
3 dead lightning bugs
4 chicken bones, picked clean
5 leaves from a dead oak tree
6 spider legs
7 pinches of red pepper
8 lumps of coal
9 matchsticks, broken in half

10 hairs from a black cat
11 toenail clippings
12 horsefly wings
13 cups of water from a scummy pond

Set the cauldron beneath the dead oak tree. Add ingredients in the order listed. Add water one cup at a time. When all the ingredients are in the cauldron, stir counterclockwise with a wooden spoon as fast as you can until a whirlpool forms. Then lightning will crackle. Thunder will boom. Wind will howl. And rain will pour down from the sky in torrents.

The two girls looked at each other and shivered.

"It . . . it must be somebody's idea of . . . of a joke," Heather said in a shaky voice. Throwing a frightened look over her shoulder, she raced toward the school, adding, "Come on, let's hurry. It's almost time for the bell." Tori stayed where she was, rereading the recipe. Tingles raced up her spine at the thought of actually following the instructions in the recipe.

"I know it sounds creepy, but what if it really is magic? Imagine how it would feel if we followed the directions and cooked up an honest-to-goodness storm?" she said excitedly when she finally caught up with Heather.

"Don't talk that way, Tori Pardo," Heather warned. Her face was so pale that her freckles stood out like measles. "I told you, it's got to be a joke. There's no such thing as magic. Nobody can make a storm just by throwing a bunch of things into a pot. And besides, which one of us is going to pull six legs off a spider? Or ten hairs from a black cat? If *you* want to do that weird stuff, *you* can make the recipe."

Heather was always sensible and she was being sensible now, Tori reminded herself. It sounded like the kind of practical joke someone like Ted Kinner would pull. Maybe she had accidentally taken her red spiral notebook to school, and he had found it. But how had he managed to erase all her secret entries? And where had he gotten a recipe for a storm?

No matter how hard she tried, Tori couldn't get the recipe out of her mind all through school that day. It couldn't work, of course, so it would be ridiculous to test it, she told herself, wishing she could be as sensible as Heather.

The funny thing was, she had a dead oak tree in her very own backyard. Her father had been talking about cutting it down for ages.

And tomorrow was Saturday, so there would be plenty of time to gather the recipe's ingredients. And figure out how to get six spider legs. And ten cat hairs. And twelve horsefly wings.

She had no intention of doing any of those

things. She reminded herself a dozen times during the day how silly the whole thing was.

When Tori got home after school the house was still. Her parents weren't home from work yet, and Max had gone to baseball practice. In her room she opened her backpack and started to pull out her social studies book to do homework. Out tumbled the red spiral notebook, landing on the floor and flipping open to the recipe for a storm.

She swallowed hard and knelt beside it, reading the list of ingredients again in spite of herself.

"Most of the things in the recipe would be easy to find around the house," she whispered. Before she knew what was happening, she was hurrying out of her room and down the stairs. She felt like a puppet, being pulled along by strings.

The garden was full of rocks, and soon she found two round smooth ones. Next she headed out to the dead oak tree in the backyard and plucked five leaves from a low branch.

Back in the house, she giggled as she sneaked her mother's soup pot from the kitchen cabinet. It would make a perfect cauldron! Then she took a bottle of red pepper from the pantry and found a box of matches in a drawer by the stove.

Suddenly what had been frightening to her before seemed like so much fun. What can be the harm? Tori wondered as she hurried to the patio where she dug eight lumps of charcoal out of the bag beside the barbecue grill.

As her excitement grew, she tiptoed into the garage. In a shadowy corner she found a dead daddy longlegs spider and a pile of horsefly carcasses. Using her fingernails like tweezers, she carefully pinched six legs off the daddy longlegs spider and twelve wings off six dead horseflies and placed them in a tissue.

At dinner that evening Tori was amazed when her mother set a plate of fried chicken on the table. In fact, she was so amazed that she didn't even mind when Max grabbed both drumsticks from right under her nose. Later, after the dishes were done, she sneaked back into the kitchen and dug four bones out of the garbage to use in the recipe.

As soon as it was dark she slipped outside and caught three lightning bugs in a jar. Next she trimmed her toenails, splitting in half the nail from one big toe to make eleven.

In the morning I'll take a bucket and a cup to the scummy pond in the park and get thirteen cups of water, she thought excitedly as she snuggled into bed. That only leaves ten hairs from a black cat—*and convincing Heather to get in on the fun!*

Chapter

The next morning Tori jumped out of bed and threw on a sweatshirt and a pair of jeans. Then she slipped quietly out of the house before anyone spotted her and wanted to know where she was going with the bucket and the cup.

A few minutes later she was holding her nose as she scooped the scummy water out of the pond and counted out each cup. ". . . nine . . . ten . . ."

Tori's hand froze in midair as a sudden chill passed through her. She shivered and looked up to see if a cloud was blotting out the sun. No. It was shining brightly. She shook away the eerie feeling and began dipping again.

". . . eleven . . . twelve . . . *thirteen!*" she said and started dragging the heavy bucket toward home.

She had to pass Heather's house on the way.

Leaving the bucket by the porch steps, she rang the doorbell.

Heather's mother answered and said Heather was in her room. Tori thanked Mrs. Hartner and took the stairs two at a time. She crossed her fingers for luck as she knocked on Heather's door.

"Come in," Heather called out. "Wow, Tori," she said when she saw her friend. "What are you doing out so early?"

"Getting thirteen cups of scummy water," Tori replied with a giggle.

"What!" cried Heather. " Oh, no, Tori Pardo! You *aren't* going to follow that stupid recipe and try to make a storm, are you?"

Tori stuck out her chin and nodded. "I've got everything I need except for ten black cat hairs. I can't wait to get started." Then she smiled sheepishly at her friend and said, "I know it probably won't work, but I just have to try. It's the most exciting thing that's happened in ages. Come on, Heather. Let's do it together," she pleaded.

Heather cocked one eyebrow and shook her head. "Why do you have to try it when you know it isn't going to work? That doesn't make sense to me."

"Who cares if it makes sense or not?" Tori grumbled. "And it won't be half as much fun without you. Besides, I need you to help me find a black cat that won't mind donating ten hairs to a good cause. Come on, Heather. Say you'll do it. Pleeeeeze," Tori begged.

"I told you I'm not interested," said Heather. "I need to work on my science report."

Tori sighed and started to leave. Suddenly she stopped and stared at Heather's bed. Half a dozen stuffed animals were piled against the pillows. One of them was a black cat with long, silky hair.

"It's fate!" Tori shrieked. She ran to the bed and grabbed the cat, holding it up in the air. "Don't you see? It was meant to be! Here's where I can get ten black cat hairs!"

"Not from my cat, you can't," said Heather, looking horrified. She took the stuffed animal out of Tori's hands and snuggled it up to her. "Do you think I want a bald cat?"

"He won't be bald," Tori said eagerly. "I only need ten hairs, and I promise I'll take them from a place that won't show. And I won't pull all of them from the same spot. Your cat will still be beautiful. Oh, please, Heather, *please!*"

"Well, I guess you can have ten hairs," Heather said reluctantly. "But I'll pull them out."

Tori watched impatiently as Heather turned the cat from one side to the other, taking one hair from here and another from there. She placed each hair in a line on her pink bedspread.

"Hurry up," Tori urged.

Heather frowned at her and kept taking her time. Finally she had ten hairs in the line. She gave the cat a final once-over and put him back on the bed.

"There, you've got your ten hairs," she said. "Now I have to get to work on my science report."

"Are you sure you won't come with me?" Tori asked one more time as she folded the cat hairs into a tissue and put it in her pocket.

She didn't want to admit it to Heather, but the spooky feeling she'd had in the park had come over her again the instant she'd touched the cat hairs. Suddenly she didn't want to be alone when she followed the recipe for the storm. "All you have to do is watch," she added in a pleading voice.

"Forget it, Tori," said Heather. "I hate thunder. And lightning scares me."

"So what?" challenged Tori. "According to you, the recipe isn't going to work anyway." Tears spurted into her eyes. "Some friend you are, Heather Hartner! You get to spend the summer in Florida while I sit at home all by myself. I'd think you'd at least want—"

"Okay, okay," Heather interrupted, letting out an exasperated sigh. "I'll come along and watch. But I'm not going to take part in any crazy scheme to cook up a storm."

The sun was shining brightly when Tori and

Heather carried the bucket of water into the backyard and set it under the dead oak tree.

"The rest of the stuff's in my room," said Tori.

The house was strangely quiet when she went inside. "Mom? Dad? Max?" she called out. "Anybody home?"

No one answered. In the kitchen Tori checked the usual spot on the refrigerator for a message. Sure enough, a scrap of paper was held to the door with a clown-shaped magnet.

Tori,
Dad and I have gone to Max's baseball game.
Home soon.
Love, Mom

It figures, thought Tori. Nobody cares what I'm doing. Max's game is too important. But at least I won't have to worry about anybody poking around and asking what Heather and I are up to.

She hurried to her room. She gathered up the red spiral notebook and all the ingredients for the storm and carried them outside. Next she set the cauldron under the dead oak tree and took a deep breath.

"Here goes," she whispered to Heather.

Heather looked nervous. She glanced first at Tori and then at the cauldron and then back at Tori. "I'm not sure I like this."

"Don't worry. I told you it'll be fun," said Tori, trying to sound braver than she felt. "Now watch." She took a rock in each hand and held them over the cauldron.

"Two . . . round . . . smooth . . . stones," Tori said solemnly. She opened her hands and the rocks clattered into the soup pot.

She picked up the jar with three dead lightning bugs in the bottom and unscrewed the cap. "Three dead lightning bugs," she said and dumped them into the cauldron.

Tori slowly went down the list of ingredients one by one. She was careful to add them in the proper order. "And thirteen cups of water from a scummy pond," she said as the twelve horsefly wings fluttered to the bottom.

She glanced back down at the recipe and gasped. "Oh, no. I forgot to bring a spoon. Wait here. I'll run back into the kitchen and get one."

Heather's eyes widened in alarm. "And leave me out here alone with this?" she said, pointing to the cauldron. "No way. You stay here, and I'll go get a spoon."

Heather didn't wait for Tori to answer. She scooted off across the yard toward the house as fast as she could go.

"Get a big spoon," Tori called after her.

Tori read over the recipe while she waited for Heather to return. Heather had been right about it being weird. Chicken bones. Spider legs. Toenail clippings. Hairs from a black cat. The list of ingredients was creepy.

"Add water one cup at a time," she whispered out loud. "When all the ingredients are in the cauldron, stir counterclockwise as fast as you can until a whirlpool forms. Then lightning will crackle and thunder will boom and wind will howl . . . and rain will pour down from the sky in torrents."

Tori shaded her eyes with her hand and squinted up at the sky. The sun was still shining brightly. There wasn't a cloud in sight.

Just then Heather came out of the house, carrying a large wooden spoon. She took her time crossing the yard to the dead tree.

"Here," she said, handing the spoon to Tori.

Tori took it. Next she grabbed the cup and started dipping water from the bucket into the cauldron. Its foul smell made her want to gag. She watched little bits of green pond-scum slide through the water and into the pot to float among the spider legs and black cat hairs and chicken bones.

When the last drop of water had been transferred from the bucket to the cauldron, Tori held onto the ladle with both hands. She stuck it into the mixture and started to stir. Round and round she turned the spoon. She was careful to keep it moving in a counterclockwise direction.

After a while her arms began to ache. Nothing was happening. No whirlpool was forming in the cauldron. No clouds were appearing in the sky.

"I guess it takes a little while to work," she said apologetically.

Heather had an I-told-you-so look on her face and didn't answer.

It made Tori stir harder. She was panting now. And the hot sun beating down on her face was making little rivers of perspiration roll down her forehead and sting her eyes.

Tori strained and stirred faster and faster. Her arms were as heavy as lead.

"Why don't you just admit that it isn't going to work and give up?" asked Heather. "The recipe's a fake. You won't make it rain in a million years."

Tori scowled and gritted her teeth, stirring even harder. She wasn't going to give up yet. Not for a long time.

Suddenly she felt a hard tug on the spoon. It was as if something inside the cauldron had grabbed it and was trying to take it away from her. She pulled back and tried to hold on, but the spoon jerked out of her hand and went spinning around in the pot by itself. As the spoon went faster and faster, the water in the center was sinking into a whirlpool.

"Look!" she shouted. "Heather! It's working!"

To Tori's horror, the whirlpool was growing bigger

and stronger and deeper as the spoon whipped wildly around, standing straight up in the water as if someone were holding it. It whipped around and around in circles, clanging and banging on the sides of the pot.

"What's happ—" Heather shrieked and jumped back. But the rest of her words were lost in a huge clap of thunder that shook the ground under their feet.

At that same instant dark clouds blotted out the sun. Lightning streaked across the sky. Wind moaned through the trees, tossing branches every which way.

Then the rain came, pouring down in torrents.

Chapter 4

Instantly Tori was soaked to the skin. She didn't care. She turned her face upward into the rain and laughed.

Her heart pounded with excitement as she shouted into the storm, "It worked! It's magic! We made a storm!"

She forgot about time, letting the beautiful rain wash over her and thinking that this was the biggest adventure of her life. She, Tori Pardo, had just made an honest-to-goodness storm! She had controlled the weather and turned a sunny morning into a rainy day! She could hear the thunder rumbling in the distance. She could feel an icy puddle rising around her ankles.

The fury of the storm was increasing with every passing second. The backyard was quickly turning into a lake. Water flowed under the gate and into the street like a river.

"Oh, my gosh, Tori! This is awful!" Heather cried over the sounds of the storm. Rain was running down her face, and her clothes were soaked. "We've got to do something."

"But *what?*" cried Tori. Looking in every direction, she suddenly realized that the storm was getting to be more than she had bargained for. "I . . . I'm scared!"

As soon as the words left her lips, thunder crashed around them. Lightning ripped open the sky, letting rain pour down in sheets.

"Try something. Anything! Look in the notebook," cried Heather. She pushed a strand of rain-soaked red hair off her forehead and looked at Tori with pleading eyes. "Maybe we overlooked a page that tells how to turn off the storm."

Tori's hands were trembling as she fumbled through the book. The rain was soaking the pages, making them hard to separate.

"Well?" demanded Heather over the sound of thunder. "Is there anything in there?"

Tori shook her head in despair.

"Come on. We'd better get into the house while we still can make it across the yard," Heather said frantically, pulling on Tori's sleeve.

"Wait!" cried Tori. "I've got an idea. What if we reverse the recipe?"

"Do you mean take things out of the cauldron in the opposite order that you put them in?" Heather asked excitedly.

Tori nodded. "It just might work." She grabbed the cup and started scooping water out of the pot. But the rain was pouring in so fast that she couldn't possibly keep up, and soon the cauldron was overflowing.

"This isn't working!" she cried. Her long dark hair was so wet that it was plastered to her face. She had to wipe it aside to see Heather.

"Why don't you just skip the water part of the recipe and pull out the other stuff?" Heather shouted. She looked anxiously at the sky. "And *hurry*! It's coming down harder!"

Tori plunged her hand into the swirling water of the cauldron. Searching frantically, she tried to catch the twelve horsefly wings. Her fingers bumped against rocks and chicken bones. They brushed oak leaves and lumps of coal, but she couldn't find a single horsefly wing.

"I can't find the horsefly wings! They're way too small!" she yelled in desperation. "And the cauldron's too heavy to dump over!"

By now the floodwater was almost up to their knees.

"Let's run for the house!" shouted Heather above the noise of the storm.

"We can't. We've got to try to stop this!" insisted Tori.

But when she looked again, the cauldron was floating away across the yard, bobbing like a cork on a wave-tossed sea.

"It's useless," said Tori, putting her hands over her ears to shut out the thunder. She began sloshing toward the back door. Heather was right beside her.

The moment they were inside the house the storm changed. Thunder rolled farther and farther away. The torrent slowed to a drizzle. Finally it stopped, and the sky lightened.

Tori and Heather looked at each other with wonder.

"What happened?" they whispered in unison.

Just then the back door flew open, and Max burst into the kitchen. He was wearing his baseball uniform. Mr. and Mrs. Pardo were right behind him. They were all dripping wet.

"Oh, Tori, I'm so glad you girls are safe," said her mother as she peeled off a rain-soaked jacket. "I've never seen such a terrible storm."

Max slammed his glove on the table and sat down, cupping his head between his hands.

"Max, what's wrong?" Tori asked when she saw the fury on his face.

"Why did it have to rain today of all days?" he

grumbled. "The best game of my whole life just got rained out."

Tori exchanged glances with Heather and asked, "What do you mean,'the best game of your life'?"

"I hit my first and only grand-slam home run, but it won't count. We had only played two innings before the storm came and they called the game," he said angrily. "You have to play five innings for a game to count. Now we have to play it over tomorrow."

"Maybe you'll hit another one tomorrow," Heather said cheerfully.

Max gave her a dirty look. "Do you know how hard it is to hit a grand-slam home run? *Impossible!*"

Tori felt a twinge of guilt. Poor Max, she thought. Baseball is his favorite game.

But she reminded herself that she had temporarily forgotten that Max was playing baseball this morning, and her guilty feeling quickly passed. She hadn't meant to spoil anything for anybody when she had conjured up the storm.

Although, Max deserved to have his greatest game rained out, she thought smugly. He was spoiling her summer, wasn't he?

"You'd better get on some dry clothes before you catch a cold," Tori's mother warned her.

She nodded. "Come on, Heather. Let's go up to my room."

The two girls trudged up the stairs. As soon as her bedroom door closed behind them, Tori spun around in a circle and shouted, "Did you see that, Heather? It was magic! I made it storm!"

"Come on, Tori. You know you didn't *really* make it storm," said Heather. "It was just a coincidence. It would have probably rained anyway. There's no such thing as magic."

"How can you say that?" Tori asked indignantly. "The sun was shining. There wasn't a cloud in the sky. Not until that whirlpool formed in the cauldron after *I* stirred and stirred in a counterclockwise direction. That was what the recipe said to do, and that's what happened! You can't deny that."

"I didn't deny it," Heather insisted. She shook her red curls defiantly. "I just said it was a coincidence, that's all. Let's face it, how could throwing a bunch of weird things into a pot and stirring them possibly change the weather? It just doesn't make any sense."

A few minutes later Heather went home. Tori changed into a dry pair of jeans and a T-shirt. Flopping across her bed on her stomach, she stared out the window and thought about her best friend. Heather didn't understand about magic. Of course it didn't make sense. But who cared. It had worked!

That was the trouble with Heather. She expected everything to make sense. Why couldn't she just do things for the fun of it? That was what had been so special about her imaginary Celeste. Since *she* had made her up, Celeste would do anything Tori wanted her to do. Even things that Tori was afraid to do herself. Like the time they went to the amusement park and rode all the rides together.

Tori had been nervous about riding the giant roller coaster called The Spiral of Death. It had the biggest vertical drop of any coaster in the state, and you could hear riders screaming two miles from the park.

Celeste had convinced Tori to ride The Spiral of Death. She had even held Tori's hand. Then when they had started down that last long drop, Celeste had stood up in her seat! Of course, since she was an imaginary friend, she was invisible. No one had been able to see her amazing feat except Tori.

Tori closed her eyes, remembering what Celeste looked like. She would look older now, but she would still have beautiful blond hair and big blue eyes—the total opposite of Tori herself.

Sometimes I wish Celeste were real, Tori thought sadly. Especially now that Heather is going away for the summer and I won't have anyone to hang out with.

Sighing, she opened the red spiral notebook and read through the recipe again. And then again. Still, she couldn't find a single clue to the magic. With another deep sigh, she closed the notebook and put it in the back of a drawer where no one would find it.

When she drifted downstairs a little while later, the television was on in the family room. She stopped to listen.

"Freak storm dumps *ten* inches of rain in only *fifteen minutes* today!"

Tori's eyes were glued to the television set as the newscaster showed pictures of some of the damage done by the storm. Streets had been closed because of flooding. Traffic was snarled everywhere. There were shots of people rowing away from their houses in boats and of cars abandoned with water up to their roofs. Everywhere things were an awful mess.

Tori scrunched down deeper into the sofa. Did *I* cause all that? she thought in horror. But how? I didn't make up the magic. I found the recipe in the red spiral notebook. *My* red spiral notebook.

Her scalp began to tingle again as the enormity of the situation began to sink in. Was someone out to get her in trouble? But who would do a thing like that? And why?

Chapter

Monday morning she met Heather at the edge of the school yard before the bell. Heather's eyes were wide, and she looked scared.

"Did you see the story about the storm on TV?" Heather asked just above a whisper. She peered around as if she was afraid someone might overhear her.

Tori nodded and started walking up the sidewalk. "Can you believe *we* made *that* happen? I mean, all we did was dump stuff in a pot and stir it."

"All *you* did," Heather reminded her. "I just watched. I didn't have a thing to do with it, remember?"

Suddenly Heather's feet flew out from under her and she went sprawling facedown across the sidewalk. Her books flew every which way.

"Owwww!" she cried.

"Heather! What happened?" Tori dropped to her knees beside Heather, who was rubbing the scrapes on her leg as tears filled her eyes.

Before Heather could answer, Ted Kinner put his hands around his mouth like a megaphone and shouted, "Hey, graceful! Walk much?"

"Yeah! Way to go, twinkle toes!" shouted Paul Meyer, Ted's best friend. They were standing together, laughing like crazy.

Tori threw them a dirty look. "Just ignore those two," she muttered. "Boys think they're so smart, but they're really immature jerks!"

Laughter was breaking out all over the playground as kids turned to look at Heather and point.

Heather's face turned fiery red from embarrassment. But when she looked at Tori, her eyes glowed with anger. "You *know* what happened, Tori Pardo! You *tripped* me!"

Tori jumped to her feet and looked down at her friend in utter disbelief. "What? I didn't trip you! How could you say a thing like that?"

"You did *too* trip me!" Heather insisted. "You stuck your foot out! I felt it!"

"I did *not!*" Tori shouted. She knew a crowd of curious kids was gathering around them, snickering and listening to them argue, but she didn't care. "That's a *lie*, Heather Hartner, and you know it!"

"Not!" Heather had gotten to her feet and was

glaring at Tori. She was leaning toward her, fists on her hips. "Not! Not! *Not!* How dare you call me a liar?"

"Because you are, that's why!" Tori retorted.

Tori stuck her nose in the air and stomped away. How *dare* Heather accuse her of sticking out her foot and tripping her? She had never felt so hurt in her life. How could Heather even think such a thing? Tori couldn't believe it. They had been best friends since third grade, and Heather had never turned on her like this before.

Tori was so hurt she didn't even look up when Heather passed her desk on her way to her seat after the bell rang.

I'm not going to speak to her until she apologizes, Tori thought.

Tori ignored Heather all morning. She sat across the room in the cafeteria at noon and made sure her back was toward Heather's table. Later, when she discovered that they were walking toward each other on the playground during afternoon recess, Tori quickly veered to the right to keep from coming face-to-face with Heather.

When the bell rang ending recess, Tori went straight to her desk without looking around for Heather. To her surprise, she found a folded piece of notebook paper lying exactly in the center of her desk.

A note from Heather. Probably an apology, she thought smugly.

Tori's injured pride wouldn't let her touch it at first. She wanted Heather to think that she wasn't in any big rush to make up. But of course she was. Her heart was breaking because Heather actually believed she had tripped her.

Finally Tori picked up the note and unfolded it, glancing down the page.

She gasped.

FOOLPROOF WAY TO MAKE EVERYONE THROW UP

Get a brown paper lunch-bag and put the following things in it:

a rotten potato
a squashed bug
three pennies
one dirty sock

At lunchtime tomorrow in the cafeteria, close your eyes, shake the bag gently, and whisper these magic words three times:

Belch, burp, barf,
Gag, retch, spew.
An awful feeling
Is coming over you.

Belch, burp, puke,
Slobber, spit, spew.
There is not a single thing
That you can do.

Tori's mouth dropped open. She forgot about all about Heather as she read the strange note.

It was written in the same handwriting as the recipe for the storm.

Chapter 7

Tori looked up from the note, glancing slowly around the classroom to see if anyone was watching. No one was.

Her mind was churning with frightening questions. Was this another magic spell? she wondered, her hands shaking. If it was, who was sending them to her? And why had she been picked as the one to do the magic?

She looked around at the other boys and girls in the room again. It couldn't be one of them. They were all just ordinary kids. So who, then? she asked herself impatiently.

Just then Heather walked by. She looked suspiciously at the note and then at Tori.

Tori jerked her hands back as if she'd been stuck by a pin. She quickly folded the note and stuffed it into her pocket before Heather could get a good look at it.

Heather gave her a disgusted look and went on to her seat.

Later, after the bell rang, Tori carefully pulled the note out of her pocket and read the message again.

Suddenly it didn't seem so frightening anymore. Just think how funny it would be if *every* single person in the entire cafeteria threw up at the same time, she thought and almost giggled out loud. Scanning the room, she pictured stuck-up, prissy Lana Byrum barfing up her socks. And Ted Kinner. He was usually the one playing tricks on someone else. He would die of embarrassment if the tables were turned.

Cool, she thought. Lunchtime was always so boring. Now it was going to be fun!

That night while Tori fixed her school lunch for the next day, she also fixed a bag for the magic spell. She shuddered as she dropped in a dead cockroach. The rest was easy.

Tuesday morning at school, she kept the bag hidden in her backpack and stared at the clock above the teacher's desk, trying to make the hands move faster.

When she got to the lunchroom, she checked out where people were sitting so that she could see their faces when she did her magic. Lana Byrum and her popular friends were at a table in the center of the room. Most of the guys from her class were by the wall, rocking backward on the legs of their chairs and laughing loudly.

We'll see how funny you think my trick is, Tori thought and smiled to herself.

She spotted Heather, sitting alone at a table near the door and felt a sudden stab of guilt. She didn't want to make her best friend throw up. Still, she reasoned, Heather deserved to throw up. She thought Tori had tripped her, even though she knew Tori would never do a thing like that.

Finally she couldn't wait one second longer. Pulling the magic bag out of her backpack, she set it on the table. She put down what was left of her peanut butter and jelly sandwich and picked up the bag with both hands.

Closing her eyes, she held it up in front of her. She shook it gently and softly began to recite the poem:

"Belch, burp, barf,
Gag, retch, spew.
An awful feeling
Is coming over you.

Belch burp, puke,
Slobber, spit, spew.
There is not a single thing
That you can do."

She whispered the poem two more times, just as the note had instructed.

Suddenly the air was filled with the sounds of people gagging and throwing up.

Tori's eyes flew open.

All over the room kids were vomiting onto their lunch trays! Teachers were throwing up into their sandwich bags! Everyone was barfing all over the tables! Upchucking onto the floor! Including Heather!

Heather gave Tori a furious look. She jumped up and headed for the door with her hands over her mouth.

A terrible stench filled the air. Tori's stomach was doing flip-flops. She grabbed her nose and rushed toward the door, too.

She stopped at the swinging doors and looked back over the scene. It was incredible! The cafeteria and everyone in it was a total mess. Tori was the only one who wasn't throwing up!

The principal dismissed school early. He made an announcement over the intercom that a sudden virus had attacked everyone at the school.

Tori laughed to herself all the way home. If only he knew!

When she walked into the house, the phone was ringing. She hurried to answer it.

"Tori Pardo, *you* did that, didn't you?" Heather demanded.

Tori cringed. "Did what?" she asked, trying to sound innocent.

"You know what I'm talking about! You made everyone throw up!" cried Heather. "That *wasn't funny!*"

"I didn't have anything to do with it," protested Tori. "Honest. It must have happened just like the principal said. You know, a virus."

"Then why were you the only one in the whole place who didn't throw up?" demanded Heather.

"I got sick, too. Only I just gagged instead of throwing up. Honest."

Tori held her breath. She hated to lie to Heather, but she couldn't take a chance on Heather telling the other kids at school about her magic. The best thing to do was to convince Heather that she was wrong.

"I think there's something fishy going on," Heather grumbled. "First the storm, and now this. I know you're up to something, Tori Pardo. You'd better watch out. You're going to get yourself into a lot of trouble!"

After Heather hung up, Tori went to her room and stretched out across her bed to think. She hated having Heather mad at her. And she hated lying. But she couldn't help it. The magic was too exciting! Besides, it suddenly occurred to her that she didn't really want to spend time with Heather anymore, anyway. She wanted to be alone. So she could think about the exciting new adventures she was having.

"Maybe Heather's going away for the summer isn't such a bad thing after all," she whispered to herself.

Chapter

Tori had barely reached the playground the next morning when she saw Heather. She was standing under a tree and watching Tori come toward her. As Tori got near, Heather picked her books up off the ground and started to meet her.

"Rats!" Tori mumbled under her breath. "I don't feel like talking to her right now."

"Tori, can I talk to you for a minute?" asked Heather.

Tori shrugged and grumbled, "Sure. Why not?"

Heather hesitated, fidgeting nervously. Finally she took a deep breath and said, "I've been thinking about what happened Monday. You know, when I fell down."

"Of course I remember," Tori snapped and

frowned. "That was when you accused me of tripping you."

"Yeah, well, I've been thinking a lot about that, and I know I was wrong," Heather admitted. "I mean, you're my best friend. You would never do a thing like that."

"Of course I wouldn't," said Tori. Her frown softened a little.

"I mean, it *felt* like somebody tripped me," Heather went on. "I don't know what it was that made it feel that way, but I should have known it couldn't have been you. I'm sorry I accused you."

Tori's heart swelled. "Gosh, Heather. I'm glad you figured that out." She hesitated. "I'm sorry, too. You know . . . that I called you a liar."

"Do you think we can be friends again?" Heather asked.

"Of course we can!" Tori said.

She felt strangely relieved. She couldn't explain why it felt so good to make up with Heather, but it did. Just because she didn't love excitement the way Tori did, didn't mean she wasn't a good friend. Tori thought about how angry she had been and felt puzzled. They had been best friends for so long. How could they have had such a big fight over something so small?

The two girls walked hand in hand toward the school.

"Hey, Pardo. How come you were the only one in the whole cafeteria who didn't upchuck yesterday?" shouted Ted Kinner. He was near the ball diamond, bouncing a baseball in his hand.

Tori stiffened. "I did too get sick," she lied. "You just didn't see me."

"Oh, yeah?" Ted said with a sneer.

"Come on, Heather," Tori said out of the corner of her mouth. "Let's get out of here."

The two girls hurried into the building and ducked into the girls' bathroom. It was still a few minutes until the bell, and the room was empty.

Tori leaned against the door. Ted had surprised her. She hadn't thought anyone had noticed. They had all been too busy throwing up! Now she was worried. If Ted Kinner had seen that she was the only one in the whole cafeteria who hadn't barfed, had other kids noticed, too?

She glanced at Heather's reflection in the mirror. Her face was serious again.

"I was right. It *was* more magic, wasn't it?" Heather asked, returning Tori's gaze in the mirror.

Tori's mind raced. What could she say? It wouldn't do any good to lie. Heather had been there when she made the storm. She would never believe Tori if she denied it.

"I found this note," she said, turning to look directly at Heather. "It was on my desk when I came in from recess Monday afternoon. Here. You can look at it if you want to," she offered. She pulled the folded piece of notebook paper out of her backpack and handed it to Heather.

Heather unfolded it and read the note slowly. A frown spread over her face. So *that's* how you did it," she said, shaking her head in disbelief. "You put all this stuff in a lunch bag and repeated this disgusting poem. Phew!"

"You won't tell anybody, will you?" Tori asked anxiously.

She held her breath as Heather stared hard at her.

Finally Heather said in a deadly serious voice, "Tori, this is scary. I don't think you know what you're getting yourself into. You're getting carried away, and *anything* could happen. Even something really bad. You ought to tear those magic spells up and throw them away!"

"It's *okay,*" Tori insisted. "I know it is! You've got to believe me! It's just for fun. Honest."

"Fun? Huh!" Heather said and scowled. "Do you realize how sick I was for a few minutes yesterday? I couldn't stop barfing! I certainly don't consider making everybody—*including your best friend*—sick as a dog very much fun! And think of the people who got flooded out of their houses. Do you call that fun?"

Tori stared at a crack in the floor. "You're right," she said. "I guess I wasn't thinking about how everybody else would feel. All I could think about was how exciting it would be to make a storm and how funny it would be if everyone threw up."

"You've got to promise me that no matter what happens you won't do any more magic spells," said Heather.

Part of Tori knew she should promise, but part of her didn't want to. The spells were the most thrilling things that had ever happened in her whole life. They were real, honest-to-goodness magic! It made her feel so powerful!

But what if Heather was right and something really bad actually did happen?

"Come on, Tori. You've got to promise," Heather insisted.

Tori took a deep breath. "Okay," she said in a small voice. "I promise."

Heather raised an eyebrow and gave her a skeptical look. "Cross your heart and hope to die?"

Tori shuddered as a sudden chill went through her. When she spoke, her voice was barely above a whisper.

"Cross my heart and hope to die."

Chapter

The following Monday, everybody was still talking about the strange virus that had attacked everyone at school. Nobody else said anything to Tori about being the only one in the cafeteria who didn't throw up.

She sniffed the air when she went into the lunchroom at noon. Although several days had passed, she thought she could still detect the faint smell of vomit lingering in the air along with the strong aroma of disinfectant.

"I'm really glad you promised not to do any more magic," Heather said on the walk home.

"Who knows if I'll ever find any more magic spells anyway," Tori responded. "I mean, it had to be just a coincidence that I found those two. No one we know could have powers like that."

Heather nodded. "Right. But you've got to admit it's spooky."

They said good-bye at Tori's corner, and Tori scuffed on down the sidewalk toward home, feeling humongously depressed.

Heather's doing what she thinks is right, Tori told herself. The trouble is, she doesn't know how I feel. She doesn't understand how terrible it can be to be lonely and that her going away for the summer is going to be awful for me. So what if I've found a special way to have a little fun?

But you promised, a little voice inside her head reminded her.

Tori pulled letters and a couple of fliers out of the mailbox on her way into the house. As she tossed them onto the hall table, the letter on top caught her eye. It was addressed to her.

That's strange, she thought. I never get any mail.

She looked closer at the envelope and gulped. She recognized the handwriting!

Tori grabbed the letter and flew up the stairs. She closed her door behind her, leaned against it, and stared at the envelope.

It *was* the same handwriting!

Tearing it open with trembling hands, she pulled out a folded sheet of notebook paper. Her heart was pounding as the words danced in front of her eyes.

Dear Tori,

If you want to find out who I am, follow these instructions:

—Put one cup of grease into a bowl. Blow in three dandelion puffs and a pinch of dust. Stir together until smooth.

—Apply this ointment to your face and arms two minutes before midnight. Then go to the dead oak tree and spread your arms out wide.

—Twenty lightning bugs will come for you and lead you up into the sky. Follow them, and they will bring you to me.

Tori sucked in her breath and stared dumbfounded at the letter. Then she read it again. And again.

"I can't believe this," she whispered. "If I follow these instructions, does it mean that I'll meet the person who's behind the magic spells? Does it mean that—*that I'll fly?*" Her eyes were wide with excitement.

But then Tori remembered her promise to Heather. She had crossed her heart and hoped to die if she ever did a magic spell again.

"But Heather doesn't *understand*," she insisted out loud.

She read the letter one more time. Her heart was aching.

"I could fly!" she whispered, the words sending shivers up her spine. "I know I could. The other spells worked. This one will, too!"

Tori stuck the letter out of sight under her pillow and tried to do her homework. She couldn't. Her eyes were constantly drawn to the soft mound at the top of the bed. It felt as if her pillow were calling to her—stealing her mind and making her think about the letter instead of her homework. Making her dream about flying.

Finally she couldn't stand it any longer. She sat up straight and pushed out her chin defiantly. "I'm going to fly, and Heather Hartner can't stop me!"

Next she searched her room until she found a pinch of dust in one corner. She put it into the envelope her letter had come in and then hurried to the backyard to collect three dandelion puffs.

Tori lay stiffly in her bed that night, staring at the illuminated dial of her clock and watching the minutes crawl by. Finally she heard her parents go to bed and the house grow silent. But it was only ten thirty!

Ten forty-five. Ten forty-six. Ten forty-seven. Was time slowing down?

Eleven o'clock finally arrived, and Tori crept out of her bed and tiptoed downstairs to the kitchen, carrying the envelope containing the dust and dandelion puffs.

She stood by the light switch for a moment, afraid to turn on the light. What if her parents saw it and came down to see what she was doing? Or what if Max heard her and started a ruckus?

An instant later she flicked it on. She would have to take the chance. Without it, she'd never be able to see well enough to mix the recipe.

As quietly as a mouse, she measured one cup of shortening into a bowl. Next she blew in each dandelion puff and the pinch of dust. Then she mixed it all together, turned off the light, and sneaked the bowl back up to her room.

She was ready. Now all she needed was for the hands of the clock to reach midnight.

Slowly, slowly, they marched toward the magic hour.

At a quarter to twelve, Tori skinned off her sleep shirt and pulled on jeans and a tank top. At ten minutes to twelve, she stuck her feet into her oldest and most comfortable sneakers. And at two minutes to twelve, she smeared the ointment over her face and arms.

At one minute to twelve, Tori slipped out of the house. Moving as smoothly and silently as a shadow, she made her way to the dead oak tree in the middle of the backyard.

She held her breath, tingling all over with excitement. It was a perfect night. The face in the moon smiled down at her, and zillions of tiny stars winked overhead.

Suddenly some of the stars grew brighter. And came nearer. Twenty of them, dancing before her eyes.

"The lightning bugs!" she whispered in awe.

Tori spread her arms and felt the ground fall away beneath her feet.

Chapter

Tori rose into the night sky, gliding through the air with the grace of a bird. Gentle breezes caressed her face and rippled her hair and clothes.

At first it felt weird. Giggling, she wiggled her feet to make sure they weren't still planted firmly on the ground. They weren't! She was flying! *She was flying!*

Over the dark landscape she soared, following the twinkling fireflies. Streetlights made occasional pools of light below, but the houses were all dark. Everyone inside was asleep.

But *I'm* not asleep! Tori thought happily. I'm a bird! I'm a plane! It's awesome! Poor sleeping people. I'll bet they'd rather be me!

She kicked her feet happily, rolling from side to

side. Next she turned over on her back, locking her hands behind her head and smiling up at the stars.

"This is *easy!*" she squealed and did a looping somersault in midair. "And cool!"

The lightning bugs led her on a zany course, zigzagging around the few tall buildings and nose-diving so close to the fountain in front of the courthouse that Tori felt spray on her face. After a while they leveled off and slowed their flight.

Tori squinted into the darkness ahead. As she came close to the ground, she could barely make out the park in the distance. The benches along the path. The swings. The slides. The seesaw. Spooky black shadows against a blacker landscape.

Suddenly her feet touched the grass. In the blink of an eye she was standing beside the scummy pond where she had gotten water to make the storm. A shiver passed through her. The fireflies were gone, and she was alone in the midnight quiet of the park.

Tori's own breathing was the only sound she heard. But as her eyes adjusted to the darkness, she could make out a figure standing in the shadows of a nearby tree.

It motioned to her.

She jumped in alarm.

"Don't be afraid," a girl's voice called out.

Tori didn't know whether to do as she was told, or to turn and run for home as fast as she could.

"Please," said the girl. " I won't hurt you. I promise. Besides, you know me. You've known me for a long time."

Tori wanted to run, but she couldn't. She took one cautious step toward the girl and then another. As she got closer, she could see that the girl was about her own age, but her face was still in shadows.

Tori stopped. Her heart was in her throat. "Who are you?" she called out. "I *don't* know you."

As Tori spoke, the girl stepped out of the shadows.

"Celeste!" Tori cried. Then she blinked in disbelief. "Celeste, it's impossible! It can't be you!"

"Of course it's me," said Celeste with a giggle. She was smaller than Tori, and delicate, with wavy blond hair curling around her shoulders. When she giggled, it sounded like the tinkling of bells.

Tori slowly backed away, her heart racing. "But it can't be you. You're not real. I made you up in my imagination. I . . . I want to go home," she said in a trembling voice.

"It's okay," Celeste said softly as she stepped toward Tori. "Don't be afraid. Now I'm really your friend. And you and I are going to have wonderful adventures. The kind you're always dreaming about."

"But . . . but," Tori fumbled for words. "How did you . . . I mean . . ."

"I'm here because you need me again," said Celeste.

Her ice-blue eyes held Tori's gaze and sent shivers down her back.

"I'll have to admit that at first I was hurt when Heather came along and you forgot all about me," Celeste went on, an edge of anger in her voice. "After all, I was your very best friend. The one you told your secrets to. And you just deserted me, as if I'd never existed."

Tori stared at her imaginary friend in horror. Surely this was a dream. Celeste *couldn't* be real flesh and blood. She had never existed anywhere except in Tori's imagination.

Celeste's expression slowly changed back to a smile. "All this time I've been waiting for you to need me again. I've been collecting my power, getting stronger, so that we could have wonderful, magical times together. Better than anything before. I'm so excited now that Heather's going away for the summer. I couldn't wait until she left to contact you. I had to do it *now!*"

Celeste's smile grew bigger. "Did you have fun making the storm?" she asked eagerly.

"Sure," said Tori, relaxing a little. "It was cool. Except—"

"Except what?" Celeste asked impatiently.

"Oh, nothing. I guess I was just thinking about the

damage from the rain," she admitted with a shrug. "Not everybody thought the storm was fun. And not everybody at school was thrilled about throwing up, either."

"Oh, don't be silly, Tori," Celeste said, making a face. "It was all just in fun. Really it was! And what about flying? How did you like that?"

Tori smiled at the memory. "That was totally cool."

Celeste threw back her head and laughed. "I thought you'd like that," she said. "It's one of my specialties."

A shadow crossed Tori's mind. "Can I ask you a question?"

"Sure," said Celeste.

"How did you get to be real? And how do you *do* those things? I mean, aren't they, well, aren't they magic?" Tori asked just above a whisper.

Celeste smiled mysteriously. "Don't worry about any of it," she said. "Just trust me. We're friends, aren't we?"

Tori nodded. "What are we going to do next?"

Celeste tilted her head and looked thoughtful. "I haven't decided yet, but I *promise* you it will be fun. Get a hall pass to the girls' bathroom during the last period tomorrow. You'll find out then. And don't forget, it's *our* secret. Just yours and mine."

Tori was about to burst with excitement. She

didn't understand how Celeste had become a real girl, or where she got her secret power. But suddenly it didn't matter. Celeste was an *incredible* friend. And tomorrow she would learn a new magic spell. They were going to have *so* much fun together!

"Please, Celeste, can't Heather come along this time?" Tori begged. "Oh, please. We could all three be friends. It would be so much fun."

Celeste's eyes blazed. "You don't need her anymore!" she spat out. "You have me!"

Tori was startled by her outburst. "I know I have you. And that's why I want Heather to meet you, too," she insisted. "I know you'd like each other."

Celeste's eyes narrowed. "Who's more fun? Heather or me?"

"Well, you are, of course," said Tori. She hadn't meant to make Celeste mad. "I only thought . . ." Her voice trailed off.

Celeste had disappeared, leaving her alone in the eerie park.

"Celeste?" she whispered into the darkness.

No one answered.

Suddenly the lightning bugs were flitting around her again like a twinkling shower.

Tori spread her arms and followed them up into the sky.

When Tori awoke the next morning, she rubbed sleep out of her eyes and thought about her awesome night. Had she only dreamed that she had flown? She could still feel the wind in her face as she soared above the rooftops, almost touching the clouds.

Suddenly she sat up and frowned. Celeste! She hadn't been a dream. Or had she? She had seemed real. She had looked exactly like the imaginary friend Tori had dreamed up so long ago. But that had just been pretend. The girl she had seen in the park last night had been more than just a figment of her imagination.

Tori gazed around her room. And if I really flew, how did I get back here? she wondered. She racked her brain. She could remember lifting off from the grass inside a cloud of twinkling lightning bugs, but she couldn't remember the flight home. Or changing back into her sleep shirt. Or crawling into bed.

"It must have been a dream," she murmured.

Tori was still at the breakfast table puzzling over her midnight adventure when the phone rang.

"Nobody move! I've got it covered!" shouted Max. He jumped out of his chair so fast it tipped over and clattered to the floor. Grabbing the receiver from the wall phone above the sink, he yelled into it, "Hello. This is Pardos. Max speaking."

Tori's mom and dad both looked up expectantly, but Max scowled and turned to Tori. "It's for you. It's Heather's mom."

"Heather's mom?" repeated Tori. "I wonder what she wants."

She took the phone from Max. "Hello? Mrs. Hartner?"

"Hi, Tori. I'm sorry to call you so early, but Heather's had an accident, and I wondered if you'd bring her homework to her this afternoon."

"Sure, Mrs. Hartner. What happened to Heather?"

"It's strange, but she fell and broke her arm in the middle of the night," Mrs. Hartner said. "Heather told us she got up at midnight to go to the bathroom. That's the strange part because she never gets up in the middle of the night. Anyway, at the top of the stairs she said her feet suddenly slipped out from under her and she tumbled all the way down to the bottom. We heard the noise and found her lying there. It was just awful."

"Gosh, that's terrible," said Tori. "How's she feeling?"

"She's okay, but she's in a lot of pain right now. We took her to the emergency room, and the doctors set her arm and put on a cast, but she won't be able to go to school for a couple of days," Mrs. Hartner continued. "I know seeing you would make her feel better."

"Don't worry, Mrs. Hartner. I'll bring her the homework, and I'll be over right after school to see her," Tori assured her.

Midnight, Tori thought as she hung up the phone. That was the exact time when I started to fly. And I promised Heather I wouldn't do any more magic.

But that wasn't all. Celeste had gotten angry when Tori asked if Heather could join the magic. She had acted jealous.

Tori shook her head slowly. Heather's accident couldn't have anything to do with Celeste, she thought stubbornly.

All day long at school Tori thought about Celeste. Her mind was churning with questions.

How did Celeste turn into a real girl? Or had Tori dreamed the whole thing? The lightning bugs? Flying at midnight? Meeting Celeste in the park? And if she hadn't dreamed up Celeste, would she be waiting in the girls' bathroom last period?

The hands trudged slowly around the clock, and the last period of the day finally came. Tori waited until her teacher, Mrs. Franklin, finished writing the math assignment on the board, and then she raised her hand.

"Yes, Tori. What is it?" asked Mrs. Franklin.

"May I have a pass to the girls' room?"

Mrs. Franklin nodded and scribbled the time, Tori's name, and her destination on a small piece of paper.

Tori took the pass and hurried into the hall. She walked quickly toward the girls' bathroom. The empty halls seemed strangely quiet without all the kids rushing back and forth. Her footsteps echoed loudly.

She stopped once and turned to listen. Had she heard someone else's footsteps, too?

Maybe it's Celeste! she thought. She looked deeper into the shadows.

Standing still in the silent hall with her ears pricked to catch the slightest sound, she felt terribly alone. She took a deep breath and tiptoed on.

The heavy door groaned as she shoved it open and stuck her head inside.

"Celeste?" she called softly.

No one answered.

"Celeste? Are you in here?" she called more loudly.

Still no answer. Tori swallowed hard and stepped inside.

Glancing at the mirror above the sink, she did a double take and read the message written in soap.

1 cup mud
6 spiderwebs
2 handfuls of grass

Mix well to form a paste.
Come to school early tomorrow and make an X on each desk in your room with the paste.
P.S. Wash off mirror as soon as you read this.

Chapter

Tori peered around the silent bathroom. Ghost fingers tiptoed up her spine.

"Celeste? Where are you?" she whispered.

No one answered.

Tori pushed open the door of each stall in case Celeste was playing a trick on her. She might be standing on a toilet so that her feet wouldn't show under the door. But she wasn't in any of them.

Shaking her head, Tori read the recipe over and over until she had memorized it. Then she washed off the mirror.

She had a funny feeling about Celeste in the pit of her stomach. Tori knew Heather had been right when she warned Tori not to get involved in any more magic spells. But she couldn't resist. It wasn't just that it was exciting. She couldn't help herself.

Just one more, she promised herself. Celeste had said this one would be fun. After that she would refuse to go along with anything weird. She wouldn't take any more chances on something bad happening—even if it meant spending the whole summer alone and miserable.

She dried her hands on a paper towel and hurried back to class. Mrs. Franklin gave her a stern look when she slid into her seat.

Tori glanced up at the clock over the teacher's desk. She was shocked to see that she had been gone fifteen minutes. No wonder Mrs. Franklin looked angry.

When Tori got to Heather's house after school, Heather was sitting up in bed, reading a book. The arm with the cast was propped up on a pillow.

Tori knocked gently on the half-open door. "Hi, Heather."

Heather dropped the book and grinned. "Wow, am I glad to see you! I hate missing school. Tell me everything that happened today, and don't leave out a single thing."

Tori rolled her eyes toward the ceiling. "Boring, boring, boring, and there's still almost two more weeks until summer vacation," she said, sitting down on the corner of Heather's bed.

Heather flounced her curly red hair and frowned at Tori. "Come on, Tori. *Something* must have happened. Nothing could have been as boring as lying in this bed all day."

"It was dull, dull, dull! Honest." She looked away so Heather wouldn't see she was lying. She couldn't tell Heather the truth. She couldn't tell her that another magic recipe was written on the girls' room mirror in soap. And she certainly didn't dare breathe a word about flying last night at midnight.

Midnight. Her mind stubbornly kept going back to the fact that Heather had had her accident at exactly the same moment Tori had started to fly. And she couldn't erase from her mind the look on Celeste's face when she had brought up Heather's name. It had been as if Celeste was jealous of Heather.

"Tell me what happened last night when you fell," asked Tori.

"It was really bizarre," Heather said, screwing up her face in a puzzled frown. "I mean, I never get up to go to the bathroom in the middle of the night. Never. And when I woke up last night, I didn't actually have to go. I don't know. I just knew I was supposed to get out of bed and go to the bathroom. I guess I must have been dreaming."

Heather paused, and Tori's heart skipped a beat.

"And?" she urged.

"Anyway, that's what I did," said Heather. "Only when I got to the top of the stairs, I felt my feet slip out from under me. It was . . . it was like a rug had been pulled out from under me. I felt myself fly into the air and then I went crashing down the stairs. The doctor said I was lucky that all I did was break my arm. He said it could have been a lot worse."

Tori stared at the ghostly white cast on Heather's right arm. *I felt myself fly into the air,* Heather had said. *The doctor said I was lucky . . .*

"Why are you staring at my cast?" Heather asked. "Hey, do you want to sign it? You can be the first one."

Tori shook away her eerie feeling. "Sure," she said, smiling. "I'd be mad if you let anyone else sign it first."

She pulled a red Magic Marker out of her backpack and signed her name, making smiley faces in the O's.

When she got home, she fell across her bed and stared at the ceiling. But instead of the ceiling, her mind saw the recipe that had been on the mirror.

1 cup mud
6 spiderwebs
2 handfuls of grass

Mix well to form a paste.
Come to school early tomorrow and make an X on each desk in your room with the paste.
P.S. Wash off mirror as soon as you read this.

Tori tried to brush away a strong feeling of foreboding.

I can't do another magic spell, she thought. Not if there's a chance that the terrible things happening to Heather have anything to do with the magic.

"Don't be silly," Tori told herself aloud. "There couldn't be any connection."

This was the first time Celeste had given her a recipe and hadn't told her what would happen when she made it. She couldn't help being curious.

"Just one more time," she whispered under her breath.

She got up off her bed and headed for the backyard to get a cup of mud.

Chapter

The school yard was totally deserted when Tori got there on Wednesday morning. No yellow buses were lined up at the curb. No kids were standing around in groups or playing on the swings. Only a few teachers' cars were in the parking lot. Tori reminded herself that it was awfully early.

Max had still been in his pajamas, staring dreamily into his cereal bowl, when she had bounded into the kitchen fully dressed. She told her parents she had to go to school early to work on a special project.

Actually I was telling the truth, she thought gleefully. This is a very special project. And all of her doubts about Celeste had evaporated like the morning dew.

She darted out of the house before her parents could ask too many questions.

Wind rustled the trees as Tori looked around the silent playground. Maybe Celeste will show up this time, she thought hopefully. But the small blond girl was nowhere in sight.

Tori had found an empty yellow margarine tub in the recycling bin in the garage and had mixed her magic recipe in that. Now she pulled it out of her backpack and headed for the school. She took one more look around for Celeste before she opened the door and went inside.

A few teachers were already in their rooms preparing for class as she tiptoed down the hall toward her room. None of them saw her. Turning the last corner she suddenly had a horrible thought.

What if Mrs. Franklin is already here, too?

Tori stopped and looked cautiously down the hall. The door to her room was open, but no light was on. That had to mean the room was still empty.

Streaking toward her classroom, she ducked inside. She breathed a gigantic sigh of relief to find herself alone and instantly set to work, smearing a small X on the first desk with the disgusting dark-brown mixture. She worked quickly, but when she got to her own desk, she stopped. If only she knew what was going to happen with this magic. Should she put an X on her desk and take a chance on whatever it was happening to her?

She thought about everybody throwing up in the

cafeteria. She was glad she hadn't been a part of that trick. But surely this one wouldn't be anything really bad. Celeste had promised her fun, not disaster. And Ted Kinner might be watching her again and see that she was the only one not affected by the magic. Quickly she smeared an X on her own desk and then scurried on to finish the others.

By the time she had gone to the girls' room to wash her hands and throw away the empty yellow margarine tub, boys and girls had started to arrive at school.

She walked around the playground in a trance. Now that she had carried out the instructions of the new magic spell her heart pounded with fear over what might happen. It could be anything. The school could blow up, for all she knew.

"So how's Heather?"

The question startled her, and she jumped a foot.

Marcie Greene was standing beside her. "Tori? Are you okay?" she asked.

"Yeah, I'm fine. Just thinking about something." Tori fumbled for words. "Heather's great. The doctor says she can come back to school tomorrow."

Suddenly a shrill ringing filled her ears. She jumped again. It was only the bell.

This is it, she thought nervously. Time for the magic show.

Tori hung back, waiting until almost everyone was in the room before she went in. Everything looked okay. Kids were going to their seats the way they did every morning. Mrs. Franklin looked normal, too.

The magic wasn't working. At least not yet.

Tori slid into her seat. Her pulse pounded in her ears. It could happen—whatever it was—any second now! What kind of magic show would it be?

But nobody seemed to be noticing the Xs on their desks. She glanced down at her own desktop and stared at the brown streaks. Muddy blades of grass stuck out every which way. It looked awful.

"Good morning, boys and girls," said Mrs. Franklin, the same way she said it every morning. "Get out your language books, please."

Desk lids raised all over the room. Then suddenly the sound of *ohs* and *ahs* filled the air.

Tori's eyes popped open as gorgeous bubbles began floating in the air! Huge soapy bubbles were floating toward the ceiling. They were filling the room, glowing with prisms of pastel light!

She threw her own desk open and caught her breath as more bubbles exploded into the air.

"Look! Aren't they beautiful?" cried Amber Delaney. She reached up to catch a shiny, sparkling bubble. Instantly it burst in her hand.

At the front of the class, Mrs. Franklin stood with her mouth open. "What . . . where . . . ?" she gasped as she turned her head first one way and then another, staring in awe.

Tori's heart was singing. It was good magic! Beautiful magic! And so much more exciting than dumb old language period! Celeste had done it again! How could I have doubted her or been afraid this spell would be anything bad? Tori wondered in amazement. She couldn't help laughing out loud.

Hands were raised all over the room, grabbing for bubbles. Kids were chasing bubbles, blowing them higher into the air. Even Mrs. Franklin seemed to be having a blast. She was trying to balance a big fat bubble on the end of her finger.

But suddenly the bubbles began to change. Tori watched in astonishment as they got smaller and thicker, lumping together like soapsuds and fountaining out of the desks. Flowing onto the floor! Piling up under the desks like snowdrifts!

"Look, everybody! I'm skiing!" shouted Paul Meyer. He jumped up and slid down the slippery aisle between two rows of desks.

Pandemonium was breaking out everywhere. Amber Delaney grabbed a handful of suds and smeared them on Tori's arm.

Tori giggled and smeared some on Amber.

"Look at this!" someone shouted, and a handful of suds the size of a snowball whizzed through the air.

The next thing Tori knew, everyone was laughing. Half the boys in the class were lobbing suds at each other as if they were having a snowball fight. A few other kids tried to slide like Paul and went crashing to the floor, knocking one another over like bowling pins. Others fell on purpose and slid into the pileup.

"Check me out! I've got rabies!" yelled Ted Kinner. He had slopped foam all over his face, and he was barking and snarling like a mad dog.

The slippery suds were getting deeper. They were rising higher and higher until they reached Tori's waist. She jumped up onto her desk and looked out at the sea of white. Other kids climbed onto their desks, too.

"Children! Stop this at once!" Mrs. Franklin shouted above the noise. Puffs of suds lay in her hair and clung to her clothes as she stood knee-deep in bubbles.

Nobody listened.

"Boys and girls! I demand that you get back in your seats!" she yelled and then blew a gob of white foam off the end of her nose.

Tori was doubled over with laughter. I love you, Celeste! she thought gleefully. This is the best magic ever!

Suddenly the door to the room burst open, and Mr. Doursley, the school principal, stepped inside. He was as big and as wide as a bear, with shaggy dark hair and a drooping mustache.

"I demand to know what's going on in here!" he boomed.

A deathly silence fell over the room.

That same instant the fountains of foam stopped flowing out of the desks. The bubbles began to burst one by one. The snowbanks of suds started to shrink.

Tori couldn't believe her eyes. No one moved. No one said a word. They watched in awe as every last bubble disappeared into thin air.

Chapter 14

The principal called each student in the class to his office in alphabetical order. Tori Pardo was near the end of the list. Mrs. Franklin assigned silent reading while the students filed in and out of the room one by one. Tori opened a book, but she was too nervous to read.

"Man, he gave me the third degree," said Josh Ackerman when he returned to class. He had been the first one called. "He thinks somebody played a trick. He's going to find out who it was if it kills him."

Tori swallowed hard and scooted lower in her seat, hiding behind her book. What would she do when her turn came? She was a terrible liar, and she knew it. Her face always gave her away.

Betty Berkowitz was next. Pretty soon it was

Amber Delaney's turn. Amber didn't say anything when she came back in the room. Instead, she raced straight to her seat, put her head down on her desk, and started to cry.

Tori tore a piece of paper out of her notebook and scribbled WHAT HAPPENED? in big letters. Then she folded it and passed it to Amber.

Amber blinked away tears and read the note. She wrote something on the paper and passed it back to Tori.

THE MINUTE I GOT IN HIS OFFICE HE STOOD UP AND YELLED, OKAY, YOUNG LADY, I WANT THE TRUTH. WHO WAS RESPONSIBLE FOR THAT MESS?

I TOLD HIM I DIDN'T KNOW, BUT I DON'T THINK HE BELIEVED ME.

The note made Tori's insides quiver. Mr. Doursley was up to the K's now. Ted Kinner had just been called.

What am I going to do? she thought desperately. He'll know I'm lying if I say I don't know anything about the bubbles. But I can't tell him the truth!

Paul Meyer was coming in the classroom door when Mrs. Franklin called out, "Tori Pardo. You're next."

Tori stood up on trembling legs and headed toward the office. What would Mr. Doursley do to her if he found out the truth? she wondered. Expel her from school? What would she tell her parents?

But the bubbles were all in fun, she argued silently. They didn't hurt anybody. And everybody loved them—including Mrs. Franklin. They're gone now, so what's the big deal? Who cares where they came from?

Tori smiled to herself. That was what she would tell Mr. Doursley. She would make him see how silly it was to look for someone to punish.

She was feeling confident when she opened the office door and stepped inside. Mr. Doursley was sitting at his desk with his back to her, talking on the phone.

The instant Tori sat down in the chair beside his desk, he whirled around and slammed down the phone. His face was a storm cloud. All her confidence vanished.

He rose slowly to his feet and glared at her. His huge bulk and his bushy dark hair made him look more like a bear than ever. A giant grizzly bear—about to attack.

Tori shrank back. She braced herself for what was coming.

The principal sucked in a deep breath and opened his mouth to speak. Suddenly his eyes grew large. He sucked in another breath. And another.

"A-A-A-CHOO!" He sneezed so hard the desk shook.

"Achoo! Achoo! Achoo!"

Mr. Doursley was sneezing so fast he could hardly catch his breath. *"Achoo! Achoo! Achoo! Achoo!"*

Tori watched openmouthed as his knees buckled under him. He grabbed at the desk as he slowly crumpled to the floor.

"ACHOO! ACHOO! ACHOO!"

Tori's heart was racing as she knelt beside him. "Mr. Doursley! Are you all right?" she cried.

He didn't answer. "A-ACHOO! A-A-ACHOO! A-A-A-ACHOO!"

Suddenly Ms. Dawson, the school secretary, raced into the room. "Mr. Doursley!" she cried. "Is something wr—" She let out a shriek.

The principal's face had turned purple. His eyes bulged. He was rolling and writhing on the floor, frantically mopping his face with a wet handkerchief.

"ACHOOOOO! ACHOOOOO! ACHOOOOO!"

Ms. Dawson grabbed the phone and punched in 9-1-1. Then she turned to Tori and shouted, "Go back to your room, and tell your teacher not to send anyone else to the office. I'm calling an ambulance!"

Tori did as she was told. She explained to her teacher and the class that Mr. Doursley was having a sneezing attack and would have to go to the hospital.

Back at her desk, she listened to the wail of the siren grow closer and finally stop outside the school.

A new fear gripped her now. Josh Ackerman's words rang in her mind. *He's going to find out who it was if it kills him.*

Had it been a coincidence that Mr. Doursley started sneezing the moment he was ready to question her about the bubbles?

Or had it been the work of Celeste?

Chapter 15

Tori went straight home after school. She knew she should take Heather's homework to her, but she couldn't face her best friend. Heather would want to know what happened at school today. And Heather would worm it out of her that the classroom had been filled with bubbles. Then Heather would get on her case for breaking her promise.

An even bigger worry was Mr. Doursley. Was he okay?

Tori paced the floor of her room after supper. She shuddered as she remembered how the principal had been writhing on the floor and sneezing so hard he could barely get his breath.

"Celeste must have put a spell on him," she

whispered to herself. "Otherwise why would his sneezing attack have happened just as he was about to ask me about the bubbles?"

Tori sat cross-legged in the middle of her bed as midnight approached. She was wide awake. Her mind was whirling. She still had a little bit of the flying ointment left. It was in a bowl hidden under her bed. Maybe it would work again, and she could fly to the park and talk to Celeste.

At two minutes to twelve she smeared ointment on her face and arms. She tiptoed out of the house and into the moonlit backyard. Wispy clouds scurried across the face of the moon. Somewhere in the darkness beyond her yard a dog howled mournfully. An owl hooted. Everything else was silent.

Tori shivered and headed for the dead oak tree. Its branches clattered in the breeze like skeleton bones. She looked up into the sky. Now the clouds had grown darker. And thicker. They were tumbling over each other. She strained to see any sign of the lightning bugs. Would they come for her tonight?

The minutes dragged by. The clouds grew even thicker until they blotted out the moon. Darkness lay like a heavy blanket on the landscape.

Suddenly something twinkling overhead caught Tori's eye. Looking up, she saw a shower of winking fireflies streaming down toward her shoulders. First three. Then six. Fourteen. Seventeen. Finally twenty lightning bugs whirled and twirled around her! An instant later she was soaring through the sky.

Celeste was standing beside the pond when Tori landed in the park. The clouds had passed now, and Tori could see her secret friend's smiling face shining in the moonlight.

Laughing, Celeste called out, "How did you like the bubbles?"

"The bubbles were great, but what about Mr. Doursley?" Tori demanded. "Did you make him sneeze?"

"He's okay. Don't worry about it," said Celeste.

"Then you did do it," said Tori. "I've heard that a person's heart stops every time he sneezes. That's scary. Don't you realize Mr. Doursley could have *died*?"

"So what if he did die? You hate school anyway," said Celeste in a pouty voice. Then she gave Tori a cocky smile and added, "Maybe they would dismiss school for summer vacation a week or so early."

Tori was stunned. "Celeste! That's an awful thing to say!"

"You're having fun, aren't you? Lighten up," said Celeste.

"Of course I'm having fun, and I want to keep on having fun. But not if it hurts someone like Mr. Doursley," retorted Tori.

"Hey, I had it under control all the time," said

Celeste. "And you have to admit, I saved you from getting into trouble."

Tori smiled weakly. "Yeah. I guess," she murmured. "And you're sure he's okay?"

"No problem," Celeste assured her.

Tori tried to shake off the eerie feeling deep inside her. Celeste had promised fun and adventure—not spells that would send people to the hospital.

"Come on, Tori," Celeste said eagerly. "Let's fly! Let's tool through the clouds like a couple of birds! I've got lots of great places to show you."

Tori glanced longingly toward the sky. She wanted terribly to do it. But . . .

"I'd better be getting home now," she said. "It's late, and there's school tomorrow."

Celeste put her hands on her hips and frowned at Tori. "It isn't *that* late. Besides, I thought you loved flying."

"I do, but . . ." Tori hesitated another instant and then said, "Okay. I'll fly, but just for a little while."

Up into the sky they soared side by side. Their arms were wide open like wings. They flew over the silent town. Wind softly caressed their faces.

"Isn't this the most fabulous thing you've ever done?" squealed Celeste. She pointed downward where buildings were as tiny as dollhouses. "Everybody down there's asleep!"

Tori couldn't help laughing. "Poor them! Look at

me! I'm a bird! I'm a plane! I'm supergirl!"

Beneath them, streetlights sparkled like jewels on a black velvet cloth. Overhead the stars twinkled brightly. They seemed so close that Tori thought she could reach out and touch them.

Her heart sang. It was breathtaking! She was swooping and rising in the sky like an eagle riding a shaft of air. She was sure no one else in the whole wide world had ever felt the way she did at that moment.

She glanced over at Celeste, gliding along beside her. There was a soft smile on her face, and her blond hair flowed over her back like golden streamers.

Celeste is okay, Tori thought. In fact, she's wonderful. So what if her tricks are a little strange? She would never actually hurt anyone. Not Heather or Mr. Doursley or anyone else!

Faint streaks of coral light began coloring the eastern sky.

"Celeste, look!" Tori cried. "The sun's coming up. We've been flying all night."

"So what?" shouted Celeste. She laughed and did three somersaults in the air. "I'm not tired. Are you?"

"Of course not!" shouted Tori. Then she did three somersaults, too.

The sky was almost light when Tori returned to her room and fell into an exhausted sleep.

Chapter 16

Tori's alarm went off like a siren a few minutes later. She dragged herself out of bed and staggered around her room, trying to get dressed. Her arms and legs weighed a ton. Her head pounded from lack of sleep. The face in the bathroom mirror stared back at her through bloodshot eyes.

"Yuck! You look gross!" Max shouted when she went down to the kitchen for breakfast.

"Thanks a lot, Max," she grumbled and sat down at the table.

"You do look a little peaked," said her mother. "Are you feeling okay, honey?"

For an instant Tori was tempted to fake being sick. That way she could stay home and catch up on her sleep. Not to mention her homework, which she hadn't done the night before. But thoughts about Mr. Doursley nagged her. She had to find out for sure if he was okay.

"I'm all right. I just didn't sleep very well last night, that's all," she replied.

It was almost time for the bell when she got to school. The first person she saw was Heather. She was in the center of a group of girls who were talking to her and looking at her cast. Amber Delaney was signing it.

The instant Heather spotted Tori, she said something to the others and left the group. Tori's heart sank. Heather was heading straight toward her with an angry look on her face.

"Just what I need," mumbled Tori. She felt grumpy from lack of sleep. The last thing she wanted was the third degree from Heather.

"Tori Pardo, what's this I hear about our classroom being filled with bubbles yesterday?" Heather demanded. "It was another one of your spells, wasn't it? And you *promised!*"

"It was no big deal," Tori said and shrugged. "It was perfectly harmless. In fact, it was cool. Ask anybody. They'll tell you how much fun it was."

"Harmless, huh? What about Mr. Doursley? He had to go to the hospital. Was that cool, too?" Heather asked angrily.

Tori opened her mouth and started to say that Mr.

Doursley's sneezing attack had nothing to do with the bubbles, but Heather cut her off.

"And don't tell me that Mr. Doursley's attack and the bubbles had nothing to do with each other, either," Heather huffed. "The girls just told me he didn't start sneezing until *you* were in his office! Explain that!"

"He's okay now," Tori said weakly. She crossed her fingers behind her back, hoping that Celeste had told her the truth.

"And you think that makes it all okay?" Heather looked at her in astonishment. Then her eyes narrowed. "Do you know something else? I don't think breaking my arm was an accident. I don't know why you did it, or how you did it, but I think it was one of your spells!"

Tori gulped. "Heather! How can you say that?" she cried.

"I told you before that I never get up in the middle of the night. And when I did that night, when I fell, it felt like somebody had pulled my feet out from under me. The *same* way it felt in the school yard that day—like someone had tripped me. And there's only one person who could have done those things. It's *you*, Tori Pardo, and you know it!"

Heather whirled away so fast that her red curls whipped around her head. Tori started to call after her. She wanted to explain about Celeste and how everything was just for fun and adventure. The bubbles had been an adventure. Everyone in the class had had fun. Even Mrs. Franklin.

But she knew Heather wouldn't believe her even if she told her the truth. Heather had no imagination. That's why she had never told Heather about her imaginary friend in the first place. Heather would never understand a thing like that. And she certainly wouldn't understand about the new Celeste and her wonderful magic spells. Tori could hardly wait to be with her secret friend again.

She scowled to herself as she thought about how dull and dreary Heather was. She let out a long, deep sigh and watched Heather walk away from her across the playground.

Tori had felt this moment coming for a long time. Now it was here. She knew she didn't need Heather anymore. Their friendship was over.

Chapter 17

Tori had never in her life hated school so much as she did that day. Her teachers were crabby. Math was boring. Social studies was boring. Language arts was boring. Even lunch period was boring. She sat by herself and watched Heather laugh and talk with a group of girls at another table.

Six more long days of school. Tori wondered how she would ever get through them. When school was out she would be able to spend all her time with Celeste. They wouldn't have to have their adventures at night anymore.

Oh, Celeste. I can't wait! she thought as she shuffled across the playground after lunch all alone.

She glanced sideways at Heather, who was sitting in the grass, talking to Marcie Greene and Betty Berkowitz.

"Just six more days," she muttered under her breath. "Then I'll be with my wonderful, fabulous, incredible best friend, the best in the world! So there!"

A sudden gust of wind rippled through her long dark hair.

"Tor-ri . . . Tor-ri, listen."

Tori jerked around. "Who said that?"

No one was there.

Frowning, she thought about the voice. It had been so soft. Like a whisper. Or had it really been a voice? she wondered. Maybe I'm imagining things.

The breeze picked up again, caressing her face.

"Tor-ri."

Her eyes widened in astonishment. It was the wind! The voice was in the wind! And it sounded just like Celeste!

"I'm listening," she said excitedly.

"Go to the dead oak tree in your backyard and dig around the exposed roots," the voice instructed. "I'll see you sooooon . . . ."

"Celeste? Celeste, where are you?" Tori cried. She twirled around, looking into the sky, but no one was there. Just as quickly as it had come up, the wind dropped. The breeze was gone.

Suddenly Tori realized that Heather and her friends were staring at her. She glared back at them for an instant and then whipped around, stomping off in the opposite direction with her head held high.

She hurried home after school as fast as she could. She didn't even stop off in the house to put down her books. Instead, she made a beeline for the backyard and the dead oak tree.

Dark roots wound around each other and wove in and out of the ground like writhing snakes. Tori shuddered and looked around for something to dig with. A broken branch from the dead tree lay in the grass nearby.

Picking it up, she poked gingerly at the soil between two of the biggest roots. Raking back the dirt, something glinted in the sunlight.

Tori dropped to her knees and began digging with her fingers, pulling out a small bottle with a medicine dropper in its cap! She turned it over in her hand.

"Oh, my gosh!" she exclaimed. "There's a note inside!"

She unscrewed the cap and pulled out a rolled-up slip of paper. Her fingers were trembling as she unrolled it.

Another spell! she thought. Her heart thudded in her chest.

Tori,

Mix one part pickle juice, one part stale coffee, and one part puddle water in this bottle. Come to the front door of the school just before dark. I'll meet you there.

Celeste

P.S. This is the best trick of all!

"The best trick of all," Tori whispered. She clutched the bottle to herself and gazed up at the sky. "I'll be there!"

Chapter 18

Tucking the bottle into the pocket of her jeans, Tori picked up her schoolbooks and went into the house. Max was sprawled out on the family room floor playing a video game. He didn't bother to look up when she passed by.

She hurried on to the kitchen to get the stale coffee and pickle juice the recipe called for. She had to work fast. Her mother would be home from work any minute.

She shook the coffeepot. There were only a few drops left. Tori held her breath, hoping it would be enough. She tipped the pot and poured it into the bottle. To her surprise, the coffee filled the bottle halfway. She dribbled a few drops into the sink so that there would be room for the pickle juice and puddle water.

Next she raced to the fridge to get the pickle juice.

"Sweet or dill?" she wondered aloud as she gazed at the two jars sitting on the top shelf. She chose dill because they were her favorite.

Even though it hadn't rained since she and Heather had concocted the storm, Tori knew exactly where to get puddle water. The outdoor water faucet near the back door leaked. There was always a small puddle underneath it.

When she had all the ingredients in the bottle, she shook it hard to make sure they were well mixed. Then she took it up to her room and set it under the lamp on her desk where she could look at it. Little tingles of excitement raced up and down her back.

"What's going to happen this time?" she whispered. She felt almost giddy. She touched the bottle with one finger to try and feel the magic in it.

"What kind of magic could come from stale coffee, pickle juice, and puddle water?"

Tori laughed and flopped back on her bed to dream about all the adventures she and Celeste were going to have. Flying a spaceship to the moon. Riding a camel across the Sahara. Chasing penguins at the North Pole. Or were they at the South Pole? It didn't matter. They would find them. Maybe she and Celeste could even become rock stars together!

It was getting late, and Tori hated to tear herself

away from her daydreams, but she had to join the rest of the family for supper. Max was obnoxious, as usual. He kept kicking her under the table and then denying it when she told on him. And her mother had fixed tuna casserole, which she hated. All in all, suppertime was pretty grim, but tonight it didn't matter.

Finally the meal was over, and it was Max's turn to help with the dishes. Tori said she had homework and went back to her room to wait for dusk, the time to meet Celeste. But the sun seemed stuck in the sky. It took ages for evening to come.

Finally the shadows in the backyard grew long and deep. The sun disappeared behind a neighbor's house and turned the fluffy clouds hanging in the sky into puffs of pink cotton candy.

Tori took a deep breath. It's time, she thought excitedly. By the time I get to school it will almost be dark.

She grabbed the magic bottle off her desk and tiptoed down the stairs. Her mother was reading the evening paper while her father helped Max with his homework in the family room.

Perfect! she thought.

She slipped quietly past without being seen. Very carefully, she unlocked the front door and opened it. A moment later she was zipping along the sidewalk toward school.

Celeste was sitting on the front steps when she got there. Even in the dusky light Celeste's blond hair seemed to glow. Her eyes were two huge pools of blue.

As soon as she saw Tori, Celeste jumped to her feet. "Come on, slowpoke," she called. "Let's go inside. We've got things to do."

Tori was startled. "We can't go in there. The school's locked at night."

"No, it isn't. See?"

Tinkling laughter filled the air as Celeste pulled open the heavy glass door and made a sweeping bow for Tori to go inside.

Tori stepped in and looked around uneasily. "We could get in a lot of trouble if somebody caught us," she warned. "They'd probably call the police."

Celeste gave her an impatient look. "Don't be silly. Nobody's going to catch us." She let the door close behind them and started down the hall. "Come on. Let's go to the office."

"The office?" cried Tori, stopping in her tracks. "Mr. Doursley's office? Why do you want to go there?"

"You'll see," chirped Celeste. "You did remember to bring the bottle, didn't you?"

"Of course," Tori replied.

She gripped the bottle in her pocket and looked around. It felt spooky to be in the empty school building at night. The moonlight coming in through the glass doors sent the girls' shadows stretching down the hallway like sprawling giants. She tried to ignore the way their voices echoed off the walls as she hurried to catch up with Celeste. She would die of fright if she was left in the dark alone.

But as she followed Celeste toward the office, her fears seemed to magically dissolve. I was silly to be worried, she told herself. Celeste won't let anything bad happen to me. She's my very best friend.

When they stepped inside Mr. Doursley's office, Celeste merely glanced at the light switch, and the light flashed on.

"How did you do that?" Tori asked in amazement.

Celeste only laughed and went straight to the principal's desk.

Tori had a sudden vision of her last visit there the day her classroom had filled with bubbles. She could see the principal slowly standing up behind his desk. He had towered over her as he got ready to yell and scream. But he never got the chance to utter a word. Celeste had seen to that. Celeste could take care of *anything*. What a friend!

"Throw all the paper you can find onto the floor," instructed Celeste. She was grabbing letters and school forms off the desk and tossing them into a pile in the center of the room.

"Cool!" said Tori. She knocked a row of books

into the pile of paper. "Let's really trash this place."

Celeste smiled brightly. "Now you've stopped being a dweeb," she said, kneeling by the books. "I'll tear the pages out of these. You start emptying out his desk drawers."

Tori didn't have to be told twice. She worked like a maniac. She pulled open drawers and pitched the contents in every direction. Everything she found that was paper got tossed onto the pile. She hummed the latest Snoop Doggy Dogg hit while she worked. She couldn't remember when she'd had such a good time.

"If Heather could see me now, she'd die," she said, laughing.

Finally all the paper had been thrown on the floor. The room was a total disaster zone. Tori looked around in satisfaction. Then she remembered something else.

"Hey, what about the stuff in this bottle?" she asked. She pulled it out of her pocket and held it in the air.

A smile lit up Celeste's face. "Shake the bottle hard to make sure it's mixed well."

Tori shook the bottle. She couldn't control the silly grin on her face. She didn't know what they were going to do, but whatever it was, she knew she was going to love it.

Celeste's eyes took on an eerie glow. "Now,

squeeze three drops onto the paper with the dropper and watch what happens," she said in a deadly serious voice.

Tori unscrewed the cap and squeezed the ball to fill the eyedropper. She held the dropper over the center of the pile of paper. Her pulse was racing as the putrid greenish-brown liquid hit its mark. Plop. Plop. Plop.

She waited, watching the liquid soak into the paper and leave dark circles.

Nothing else happened.

Tori frowned. "Did I do something wrong, Celeste?"

Celeste didn't answer. Instead she stared at the paper as if she was in a trance. Slowly she began to smile. Then she raised her hand and pointed to the drops.

Tori gasped. A tiny flame glowed from somewhere deep inside the pile of paper.

Chapter

"Fire!" Tori screamed.

She grabbed a sweater off a coatrack in the corner and beat it against the flame. "Fire, Celeste! Help me!"

Without answering, Celeste pushed Tori aside and whirled in a circle before the tiny fire, spinning and spinning and laughing wildly. The room was filled with a whirlpool of wind.

Suddenly the flame soared. Orange tongues exploded toward the ceiling and licked the wall. Waves of heat radiated from the blaze.

Tori shrank back in horror. The sweater fell from her hands.

"Celeste! What are you . . ." Her words trailed off.

Her gaze was drawn to the beautiful golden fire.

Flames danced crazily before her eyes, reaching higher and higher. She watched in total fascination as the blaze grew bigger and bigger, spreading its delicious warmth to every corner of the room.

Celeste whirled faster and faster, fanning the flames higher.

Perspiration streamed down Tori's face. Smoke rolled in the air and filled the room, choking her and making her cough.

But strangely it didn't matter. Nothing mattered but the gorgeous fire starting to engulf the room. She watched in a trance as the flames nibbled at the furniture. Devoured the curtains. Raced up the walls and licked across the ceiling.

"Oh, Celeste! I love it!" Tori cried, clapping her hands. "We're burning down the school!" She wanted to dance and sing and jump up and down. She started whirling, too, dizzily following Celeste around the fire.

Suddenly there was a gigantic cracking sound overhead.

"The ceiling's going to cave in!" shouted Celeste. "Come on!" She grabbed Tori's arm and pulled her out the door.

The halls were so full of black smoke Tori couldn't tell which way to go. Her eyes stung. She was hacking and gasping for breath.

At that instant the office ceiling came crashing

down and sent spark-filled smoke billowing out into the hall.

Celeste calmly looked to her right and to her left and then held out a hand to help Tori follow her through the black smoke. To Tori's amazement, a few seconds later they were out the front door and into the fresh night air.

Tori dropped to her knees in the grass and flopped over onto her back, trying desperately to catch her breath. Her lungs felt as if they were on fire. Each breath was torture.

Then, as her breathing became easier, she saw out of the corner of her eye a huge red glow silhouetted against the black sky. Turning, she stared in awe at the flames shooting out the windows and climbing toward the roof.

"Isn't it beautiful?" cried Tori, bouncing up and down with joy. "School's out! School's out! Teacher let the monkeys out!" she sang at the top of her lungs.

In the distance a siren screamed. As it grew louder, Tori looked around frantically for a hiding place.

"Quick! There are some bushes!" she shouted, pointing to a hedge at the edge of the school yard. "Let's hide!"

"Right!" said Celeste.

The girls raced toward the bushes, ducking behind

them just as two big red fire trucks came screeching to a halt in front of the burning school. Tori parted the leaves and peered out as yellow-coated firemen jumped out of their trucks, pulling long hoses. They quickly connected them to fire hydrants and began spewing giant streams of water on the school.

A crowd was starting to gather across the street from the burning building. People rushed out of their houses to stare and point. Passing cars screeched to a stop. Kids rolled up on their bikes.

To Tori's horror, one of them was Heather! Her face glowed, shimmering in the light of the fire. She had an eerie look on her face, and she was slowly nodding her head up and down as if she knew a secret.

A shiver went through Tori.

"You don't think Heather knows we did this, do you, Celeste?" she asked anxiously.

Celeste didn't answer. She had vanished.

Chapter 20

It was a long time before the fire was out and the firemen and the crowd had gone home. Tori was still crouched in the bushes, watching. But she wasn't really seeing what was going on. What she saw was the expression on Heather's face. It filled her thoughts and made her tremble with fear.

"Heather knows," she whispered through chattering teeth. "She knows."

The horror on Heather's face had melted Tori's excitement. It had frozen her joy.

Her stomach churned as she stared at the charred ruins of the school. What if Heather told?

But she can't prove anything, a voice in her mind whispered.

Still, Tori had an instant flash of the police banging on her door and then dragging her off to jail. Putting her in a tiny cell and throwing away the key. She looked back at the smoldering building as a new horror began building inside her.

"How could *I* do such a thing?" she murmured in astonishment. "I'm not a *criminal!* I don't burn down schools!"

Blinking, she stared at the charred walls and the blank, gaping windows of the place where she had gone to school since kindergarten. The roof had fallen in. The front door barely hung by its hinges. The smell of smoke filled the air over the playground where she and Heather had had so much fun. It stung her eyes and burned her nose.

"It was Celeste's fault! She made me do it!" Tori shouted, jumping to her feet. "She used her magic to get control of me and to get revenge for forgetting her when Heather became my friend!"

Crashing through the bushes, she began running toward home as fast as her legs could carry her. When she got there her house was dark and silent. She unlocked the back door as quietly as she could and tiptoed inside. Her bedroom door was still closed. That meant her parents thought she had gone to bed early and hadn't wanted to wake her to say good night.

Tori hadn't realized how tired she was until she saw her bed, framed in a patch of moonlight. It looked so inviting. Her head ached. Her arms and legs felt like cement. She was exhausted. Maybe if she could just lie down for a moment.

No! she told herself. I have to talk to Celeste! I *have* to! I have to make her understand that I don't want to do things like burn down the school!

Kneeling beside her bed, she pulled the bowl of flying ointment out from under it. There was only a tiny bit left. Would it be enough? She scraped the bowl clean with her finger and smeared it on her face and arms.

The digital clock on her desk said 4:18. A new worry hit her. She had always flown at exactly midnight. If she went to the dead oak tree now, would the fireflies come?

Her heart was in her throat as she looked up through the branches of the tree a moment later. She ached to be back in the peaceful safety of her room. She had had enough midnight flying adventures to last the rest of her life. Part of her wished the lightning bugs wouldn't come. But she knew what she had to do.

They came. They flickered down around her like fairy dust, sparkling in the moonlight. They twirled and whirled around her and then landed on her outstretched arms.

Tori inhaled deeply as she whooshed into the sky with the speed of a rocket. She was flying so fast that the buildings below her blurred. Wind blew her hair straight out behind her like a flag in a gale and pinned her arms to her sides. She tried to slow down, but she couldn't.

An instant later the fireflies put her down in the park. It was the spot where she always landed, near the tree beside the scummy pond.

Celeste rushed out from under the tree. Her face was glowing. "Wasn't it wonderful? Did you see those beautiful flames?" she shouted, raising her arms and spinning round and round like a Gypsy dancer. "Now school is out! We can have *real* fun!" Her laughter filled the air.

"Celeste! How can you say that? We burned down the school!" Hot tears stung Tori's eyes. "We were just supposed to have adventures! All I wanted was to do fun things! Not burn down the school! Celeste, how could you *do* a thing like that?"

Celeste's smile turned to a sneer. "Don't kid yourself, Tori Pardo. *You're* the one who did everything. You dreamed me up in your mind. I'm not just your secret friend. I'm your *imaginary* friend, remember? I've already explained to you who I am."

Tori gasped. "But . . . but I . . . I didn't mean . . ." Her voice trailed off as the terrible meaning of Celeste's words sank in.

"Oh, yes, you did. You craved adventure and excitement so badly you could hardly stand it."

Celeste spat out the words and looked at Tori through narrow slitlike eyes.

"First, when Max was born and you thought your parents were ignoring you, you felt lonely and forgotten. Next, when you had trouble finding anyone your age to play with in tiny little Domburg, you felt lonely and forgotten all over again. That was when you created me out of the energy from your mind. You dreamed me up and made me into the real live friend you couldn't find. I didn't mind. I loved the job of making sure you had a good time. And we did have fun, didn't we?"

Tori nodded in silence. Everything Celeste was saying was true.

"And you thought that when Heather came along and you didn't need me anymore that I would just disappear. That I would just stop existing. Well, you were wrong! I've been here all along, watching you give your friendship to Heather instead of to me. I've been waiting for the moment you realized that I'm a better friend than Heather could ever be. And while I was waiting, I was absorbing more and more energy from your mind. I was getting stronger and more powerful with every passing day. And now that Heather is deserting you for the summer and you need me again, I'm back."

An evil smile spread over Celeste's face. She took a step closer. Fury burned in her eyes. "Don't blame me for anything. You wanted fun. We had fun, didn't we? We made everybody barf in the cafeteria. You laughed your head off. We filled all the desks in your classroom with bubbles. You loved it. Don't deny it. We took midnight rides in the sky while everybody else slept. You liked that the best of all, didn't you?"

Tori nodded. "But what about the recipe for the storm? I didn't ask for that."

"I thought you'd figure that one out for yourself," Celeste said, rolling her eyes in disbelief. "You secretly wanted to get even with Max for joining the baseball team and spoiling your chances for an exciting summer vacation. We rained out his game after he hit a grand-slam home run. Like I said, everything I did was for you!"

"You can't mean you burned down the school for me?" Tori asked, shaking her head incredulously. Her heart was racing. It couldn't be true!

Celeste nodded angrily. "I did that for *both* of us. I couldn't wait one second longer for Heather to leave town. You couldn't wait for school to be out for the summer so that you could be with me. Well, now it is."

She threw back her head and let out a laugh. Her sinister cackle bounced through the branches of the tree overhead and ricocheted off the stars.

Chapter 21

Tori shrank back in horror. It couldn't possibly be true. And yet it was impossible to doubt it. The glow in Celeste's eyes was pure evil.

Tori backed away slowly. I have to get out of here! her mind screamed.

Suddenly she realized that Celeste had something in her hand. A doll? Tori looked closer.

"Oh, no. Oh, nooo," she moaned. It was a doll. And it had curly red hair and a cast on one of its arms. It was Heather!

Celeste's cackle filled the air again and echoed like a monster voice in an amusement park fun-house. She took the doll by one foot and shook it in Tori's face.

"We're not going to let her come between us anymore, are we? She's too *boring* to have the kind of fun we have! *Let's get rid of her!*" Celeste hopped up and down, swinging the doll around and around over her head and laughing hysterically.

Tori put her hands over her mouth and stared in horror at the doll as it swung helplessly in the air. She couldn't doubt the truth any longer. Celeste had tripped Heather on the playground. And Celeste had pushed Heather down the stairs the night she broke her arm. Celeste was growing stronger and more evil. There was no telling what she might do to Heather now.

Celeste stopped hopping around and turned to look at Tori. The doll hung limply in one hand. She rubbed her chin with the other.

"It's time to get rid of Heather. Permanently!" Celeste snapped. She took a step toward Tori, holding up the doll like a trophy. "And I want *you* to do it!"

"Oh, no, you don't," Tori said in a trembling voice. She put out her hands to keep Celeste from coming closer. "You can't make me do it! Not a thing like that!"

"Oh, yes, I can," Celeste snarled. "I've already proved to you what I can do."

She curled her lips into a sneer and took hold of the doll's head as if she were going to pull it off. "Or maybe I'll just have to get rid of Heather myself and make it look like you did it."

Tori couldn't believe what she was hearing. Celeste was going to kill Heather and put the blame on her!

Tori lunged and grabbed the doll out of Celeste's hands.

"You can't!" she cried, whirling away from her. "I won't let you hurt her!"

Instead of coming after her, Celeste reached up into the branches of the tree and pulled something out. It was another doll! And this one looked exactly like Tori!

Tori let out a scream and ran across the park, her feet barely touching the ground. She could hear Celeste behind her, laughing insanely.

Tori tried to wipe off the flying ointment as she ran. She knew she could get home faster if she flew, but she didn't dare try. The fireflies were in Celeste's power, too, and she didn't know what they would do.

Pain tore at Tori's side. She stopped once to clutch at it and to glance behind her. Celeste wasn't there. But Tori knew better than to hope she was gone. Celeste could be anywhere. In the sky above her, ready to pounce any second. Behind a tree. Lying in wait for her in her room.

As Tori started running again, dawn was painting the sky a brilliant orange. She couldn't believe that it was morning already. She had been out all night.

No one was up yet when she got home. She slipped inside and up the stairs to her room as silently as a shadow. Her heart was pounding as she cautiously opened the door and peered inside. The room was empty. Celeste was not there.

Tori staggered inside, closing and locking the door behind her. She went to her bed and gently put the Heather doll down. She wanted to collapse beside it. She ached to fall into a deep, exhausted sleep and wake up to find it had all been a dream. But she didn't dare. And it hadn't been a dream. It was terribly, terribly real.

Now she had to think of a way to save Heather from Celeste's evil clutches.

She had to find a way to save herself, too.

But how?

Tori paced the floor of her room until she heard her parents get up and head downstairs to the kitchen.

She had to get to Heather and make sure she was still all right. Hurrying to the door, she caught sight of herself in the dresser mirror and stopped. She looked awful. Dark ashes smudged her face. Her hair smelled like an old campfire. There was a rip in the knee of her jeans.

I can't let my parents see me like this! she thought. They'll know I was at the fire and ask a lot of questions.

Pulling off her clothes, she scampered across the hall to the bathroom. She turned on the faucets full blast and scrubbed the ashes off her skin. Next she ducked her head under the faucets and rinsed the smoke out of her hair.

She wrapped a towel around her head and dashed back to her room. "That will just have to do," she mumbled as she dressed.

When she got to the kitchen a few minutes later, her mom, dad, and Max were gathered around the radio. Her mother raised a hand for her to be quiet the instant she stepped into the room.

"The cause of the blaze is under investigation," the announcer was saying. "School officials have canceled all classes and dismissed students for the summer."

"Yea! Yea! School's out! School's out! Teacher let the monkeys out!" Max shouted. He bounded around the room, doing a monkey imitation. "Oooh! Oooh!"

"That's right, Tori," said her mother, frowning. "Something terrible has happened. Your school burned to the ground last night."

"*What?* Gosh! That's awful!" Tori said, trying to fake surprise. "I'd better go and see if Heather has heard about it."

She hurried out of the house before anyone could stop her and ran all the way to Heather's. Her heart was in her throat as she pushed the doorbell hard. She danced on the balls of her feet while she waited for someone to answer. What if Celeste had already gotten to Heather? What if it was too late?

Heather opened the door.

She stared at Tori in disbelief. "Go away! I don't want to talk to you!" she said angrily and pushed the door closed again.

Tori lunged at the door, keeping it partly ajar. "Heather! You've got to listen! Things aren't like you think! Please! Please let me in!"

Heather leaned against the inside of the door, trying to force it shut. "I said to *go away* and I mean it!"

Tori put all her weight against the door, pushing it partway open again. "You don't understand!" she cried. "I came to save your life!"

Heather's angry expression went blank. She stared at Tori. "What do you mean?" she demanded.

"Let's go to your room where nobody can hear us, and I'll tell you," said Tori. "Please, Heather. You've got to listen."

Heather led the way up the stairs. Every few steps she would turn around and frown at Tori. "All I've got to say is this had better be good," she muttered as she closed her bedroom door behind them. "Well?" she said, turning to face Tori.

"It's hard to know where to start," said Tori, shifting nervously from one foot to the other. "Remember the red spiral notebook? The one with the recipe for the storm in it?"

Heather nodded. "How could I forget? You nearly went berserk when I tried to look inside. But the pages were all blank except for the one with the recipe. This has something to do with all those magic spells, doesn't it?"

"Yes," said Tori.

"And you didn't keep your promise, did you?" Heather asked angrily. "And now I suppose you're in trouble."

Tori filled her lungs with air and then slowly let it out. She had to tell Heather the truth, and she had to do it now before it was too late. "You're right. I am in big trouble, just like you said I'd be," she admitted. "But it's worse than that. You're in big trouble, too."

She went on to explain about how she had meant to keep her promise, but that the next spell had told her how she could fly. And when she did, she had met Celeste, her old imaginary playmate from a long time ago.

Heather's mouth opened wide in disbelief, and she slowly moved away from Tori. "You're joking! You're not trying to tell me that your imaginary playmate suddenly came to life and started making magic, are you? Because if you are—"

"It's true! Heather, *please* give me a chance to explain. I know it sounds crazy, but she's real! And at first Celeste seemed like the most exciting girl in the world. . . ."

As she talked, Heather's eyes grew wider and wider.

"So where is this Celeste?" Heather demanded. "I've got a few things I'd like to ask her myself."

Tori gasped. "You can't! She wants to ki—" She stopped short. She couldn't tell Heather about that. Not yet. Not until she finished the whole story.

"So you see, I created an imaginary friend to have adventures with. But her magic has gotten so powerful that she's turned into a monster, and now she wants to kill us both!" Tori finished, heaving a weary sigh.

Heather hadn't said a single word while Tori spoke. Now she frowned and spat out, "Tori Pardo, you don't really expect me to believe a stupid story like that, do you? I'd have to be crazy. It's some kind of trick. And you'd better tell me how you did all those things *right now!*"

Tori started to argue. But before she could get a word out, there was a knock at Heather's bedroom door.

"Who could *that* be?" Heather let out an exasperated sigh. "Come in!" she snapped angrily.

The door opened slowly as Tori watched with horror-filled eyes.

"Hi, Heather," said the smiling blond-haired girl standing there. "I'm Celeste. You're mother said it was okay if I came on up."

Chapter 23

Celeste closed the door to Heather's room behind her.

"So," she said, smiling wickedly, "who are you two gossiping about this morning? As if I didn't know."

Then she turned on Heather. Her eyes had turned black and were glittering with an inner evil.

Tori's heart dropped into the pit of her stomach.

"No!" she cried, planting herself between Celeste and Heather. "Don't hurt her! Please! It's me you really want! I'm the one who created you!"

"Tori? Celeste? What's going on?" Heather asked in bewilderment.

Celeste ignored both of them. To Tori's amazement, she sat down on the floor and pulled off her sneakers. Then she slowly pulled the laces out of each of them. Sitting cross-legged, she draped the laces over one arm, looking first at Tori and then at Heather.

Tori's insides started to quiver. "What are you doing, Celeste?" she demanded.

Without a word Celeste stretched out each lace in a straight line on the floor—one pointing toward Tori and the other toward Heather. Then she waved a hand over each one.

Tori stared at the laces. Black smudges from where they had been pulled through the eyelets of Celeste's shoes made patterns like the markings on the backs of snakes.

"Snakes!" she gasped.

The laces were growing larger and larger and thicker and thicker! Snake heads appeared on the ends pointed at Tori and Heather. Then flickering tongues darted in and out of their mouths to taste the air around the girls!

Tori shrank back in horror. It was impossible! But it was happening. They were growing into diamondback rattlesnakes!

The snakes' heads rose up and bobbed as beady eyes sought out their prey, tongues flickering in and out of fang-filled mouths. Very slowly they began slithering across the floor toward the girls. One toward Tori. One toward Heather.

Screaming, the two girls grabbed each other, clinging together in terror.

The snakes kept coming, their deadly mouths open, their fangs gleaming in the morning sunlight.

"Mom! Dad! Help!" Heather shrieked.

Celeste's laughter echoed off the walls of the room. "They can't hear you. My magic has taken care of that. And don't think you can get out the door either. I've taken care of that, too."

"Celeste, stop them!" Tori begged. "We'll do anything you want! I promise!"

"That's right!" Heather pleaded. *"Anything!"*

Celeste threw back her head and laughed again. "Why, Tori. I thought you *liked* adventure and excitement," she said sarcastically. "Isn't this exciting?"

Tori tried desperately to answer. To beg and plead Celeste to call off the snakes. But her lips wouldn't move. Her body was numb with fright. She watched in terror as the giant snakes crept closer and closer.

Heather scrambled onto the bed, pulling Tori up with her. The rattlers were writhing toward them, hissing loudly. Suddenly they stopped.

Rolling themselves into coils, the deadly snakes reared up and trained their beady eyes on the girls. They began shaking their rattlers like a death chant.

"Hissssss," they sounded in unison.

They were ready to strike!

"I'm sorry, Heather! This is all my fault!" Tori whispered through chattering teeth. "If I hadn't wanted excitement and dreamed Celeste up, this wouldn't be happening!"

"It's okay," Heather whispered back. Tears were streaming down her face. "I know you didn't mean for this to happen," she sobbed. "We're still best friends, okay? Best friends *forever!*"

"Best friends . . . *forever!*" Tori promised.

"Best friends forever. Ha!" Celeste scoffed. "You know *I'm* the friend you've really wanted all along. You said yourself that Heather was boring. But now *I* don't want *you* anymore, Tori! *You're* the one who's gotten boring. And I'm the one with the *power!*"

Celeste's evil gaze shot into Tori so hard that she let go of Heather and staggered backward on the bouncing bed.

"No!" she said, shaking her head defiantly. She steadied herself against the wall as a sudden new thought flashed into her mind. "No, Celeste. You're wrong."

A great new feeling flooded through Tori. She knew how to defeat Celeste now. If only she had thought of it sooner.

"If my mind created you, then I can get rid of you the same way," she said in a deadly serious voice. She locked eyes with Celeste, willing her to disappear.

"Don't be foolish," Celeste spat out. "You can't get rid of me that easily. My power has grown too strong since you first thought me up."

Tori gritted her teeth with determination. "Just watch me!"

Suddenly there was a rustling on the floor.

"Hisssss!

The two giant rattlers lunged upward like twin rockets just launched. They missed Tori and Heather by less than an inch and buried their deadly fangs deep in the bed.

Tori heard Heather scream. But she stood as if frozen, her eyes locked with Celeste's.

Out of the corner of one eye, she saw the snakes grow as limp as strings and slither backward, landing in a heap on the floor.

She stared into Celeste's eyes as hard as she could.

"They're shoelaces!" she shouted. "That's all your snakes are and all they'll ever be."

The snakes' bodies began to shrivel and shrink. Their beady eyes and patterned backs faded back into dark smudges on white cotton laces. Their heads disappeared.

Tori held her breath. Shoelaces! Shoelaces! Shoelaces! she thought as hard as she could. The laces lay still on the floor like skinny strings.

Heather clutched Tori's arm. "It worked!" she cried.

"You think you're so smart," said Celeste. "Well, you aren't nearly as smart as you think you are. I can turn them back into snakes anytime I want to. That's how *powerful* my magic is."

She slowly raised her hand and pointed past Tori and Heather toward something else on the bed.

Tori jerked around and jumped off the bed. Heather's stuffed black cat had sprung to life. It arched its back and spat at Tori, swiping at her with razor-sharp claws. A long, low growl came from deep in its throat.

"I don't think it liked the way you pulled out its hair to make that storm, did you, kitty?" Celeste grinned wickedly.

Tori darted a quick look at Heather's bed and panicked. The pillows were covered with stuffed animals. Bears! Dogs! A lion! Had the lion blinked? Had one of the bears opened its mouth? Tori did a double take. Was Celeste bringing them all to life?

Whirling to face Celeste again, Tori concentrated as hard as she could. "I don't need you anymore," she murmured, looking deep into Celeste's eyes. "I made you and now I'm destroying you. You are evil.

You're never going to use your magic against anyone again."

Celeste's eyes fluttered. A frightened look spread across her face. She seemed to fade. For an instant Tori thought she could see right through her.

Then she was back, as strong as ever.

"You're weak and helpless, you and your puny friend Heather," snarled Celeste. "You'll never destroy me. I'm here to stay!"

Tori felt a breeze pick up in the room.

All the windows were shut!

The breeze changed into a gusty wind. A hot wind. Like the wind Celeste had whipped up when she whirled round and round at the fire.

But Celeste wasn't whirling now. She was standing perfectly still, her fury-filled eyes locked on Tori's.

The wind turned into a gale. The curtains whipped at the windows. Papers swirled in the air. The room was like the inside of a tornado!

"Tori! Tori!" Heather shrieked with fright. Her voice was almost lost in the roar of the wind.

Tori couldn't answer. It took all her strength to keep her eyes locked on Celeste. And all her concentration to keep repeating the words over and over in her mind:

I made you and now I am destroying you! You are evil! I made you and now I am destroying you!

Celeste slumped against the dresser. Her skin was

growing thin and pale again. Her blue eyes had now turned a milky white.

I made you and now I am destroying you! You are evil! Tori thought as hard as she could.

Celeste seemed to rest for a minute. Then she pushed herself away from the dresser.

"You can't destroy me. I'm your best friend," she said. Her voice was strong again. "You'd hate yourself. You'd be giving up excitement! Fun! Adventure!"

Suddenly Tori began to laugh. She looked at Celeste in astonishment and laughed even harder. That was it! Celeste had given her the last clue.

"Heather! Come here! Hurry!" she called.

Looking bewildered, Heather raced to her.

"Here, grab my hand," ordered Tori. "Now," she said when they were clasping hands, "let's tell her what it's like to be best friends."

"What do you mean?" Heather asked.

"Like how wonderful it is to trust each other and tell each other our deepest secrets," said Tori.

Heather nodded. "Right. And sleep-overs. And talking about boys," she added and giggled.

Tori felt a grin spread over her face. "And we have fun together in other ways, too, like going to movies and playing video games together."

"And we style each other's hair!" said Heather. "And have pizza parties!"

"But that's . . . that's boring," said Celeste in a raspy voice. She had a terrible look on her face, as if she'd swallowed a nest full of wasps. "Bor . . ." Celeste tried to say. "Bor . . ." But the words faded away like the sound of a clock running down.

Before the girls' astonished eyes, Celeste began to shrivel, like a balloon leaking air. Her mouth was opened wide with fright.

"Help!" she cried, but her voice was thin and high-pitched.

Her knees buckled and she sank to the floor, reaching a hand toward Tori. *"Tori . . . pleeease . . . pleeeeease!"* Her squeaky voice was growing faint. Her skin was so transparent that Tori could see through her!

Finally, with a gigantic sigh, Celeste faded away completely.She was gone. Just as Tori had known she would be.

"Oh, Tori!" Heather shouted. "You did it! You destroyed her! But *how?*"

Tori gazed wistfully at the spot where Celeste had been. "It was easy. I showed her the power of real friendship."

The wind had stopped now. The black cat was a stuffed animal on the bed again. The lion and bear were still. The shoelaces had magically disappeared from the floor.

Tori felt tears welling up in her eyes as she and Heather hugged tight.

"I'm not going to my grandmother's this summer," Heather announced. "I'm going to stay right here with you!"

"And we'll do all the things we told Celeste about. Hey! Let's even go to some of Max's games!" shouted Tori, bouncing excitedly on her toes.

"I can't wait!" cried Heather.

"Oh, Heather," Tori whispered despite the lump in her throat. "Having a *real* best friend is the nicest adventure anyone could ever have."

About the Author

Betsy Haynes has written over fifty books for children, including *The Great Mom Swap,* the bestselling The Fabulous Five series, and the Taffy Sinclair books. *Taffy Goes to Hollywood* received the Phantom's Choice Award for Best Juvenile Series Book of 1990.

When she isn't writing, Betsy loves to travel, and she and her husband, Jim, spend as much time as possible aboard their boat, *Nut & Honey*. Betsy and her husband live on Marco Island, Florida, and have two grown children, two dogs, and a black cat with extra toes.

About the Author